Ginger Rogers

and

The Riddle of the Scarlet Cloak

An original story featuring
GINGER ROGERS
famous motion-picture star
as the heroine

By LELA E. ROGERS

Illustrated by Henry E. Vallely

Authorized Edition

WHITMAN PUBLISHING COMPANY

RACINE, WISCONSIN

TABLE OF CONTENTS

ILLUSTRATIONS

Ginger Rogers Was at the Telephone Switchboard

GINGER ROGERS
and the Riddle of the Scarlet Cloak

CHAPTER ONE

THE INGRATIATING MR. DUNLOP

GINGER ROGERS sat at the telephone switchboard of the Seaview Arms Hotel in a city on the West Coast. One pump-clad foot tapped a lazy rhythm on the circle of wood that held together the long legs of the stool on which she was perched. Eight hours a night, six nights a week, she sat there, answering in that "voice with a smile" the thousand-and-one strange requests which only the guests of expensive hotels have the courage to make or the imagination to conceive.

The one light in the room hung over her head, shaded to share its illumination with Patsy, the only other night operator, who sat beside Ginger. The glow caught the long sweep of Ginger's dark brown hair, setting it afire with burnished lights, and made weird shadow-patterns of criss-crossed wires and elongated fingers, weaving back and forth across the face of "the board," dexterous and graceful.

The tapping foot was a sign that Ginger's heart was free, that she liked her work and knew that her efforts were appreciated by everyone, from the office downstairs to that last guest in the single room near the noisy elevator shaft. Ginger knew her hotel from basement to roof and knew how to get service to its guests in the least possible time. She knew her town and how to direct the vacationer to any place he wanted to go. After advising each such guest, she left him with a feeling that he was the most important guest the Seaview Arms had ever had the pleasure to serve.

Ginger Rogers was not the "usual" telephone operator, because the Seaview Arms was not a "usual" hotel. Built in 1926 by Madame Millinet DuLhut, a Frenchwoman, it stood in all its Spanish majesty in the midst of broad gardens, crowning the brow of the Palisades overlooking the calm Pacific. Madame's husband had owned famous hotels in Paris. When, after his death, Madame had come to America to find solace and surcease, she had decided to build the Seaview Arms to give her something to do. She knew hotel management better than anything else in the world. The Seaview Arms was Spanish in its architectural design, to fit its surroundings, but Madame had decreed that from its kitchens and staff should come only French food and service.

The Seaview Arms prospered and waxed rich. Its exquisite cuisine was famed round the world. Year after year, it gathered into its spacious lobbies, drawing-rooms and elegant suites the cream of the traveling continentals. It became THE place to go when vacationing along America's California "Riviera."

Wise and prudent Madame DuLhut had learned, through a lifetime spent in hotel management, that the girls who were to sit at the Seaview Arms switchboard must be chosen with great care. She was well aware that the switchboard was the heart and voice of her hotel and that its girls had the power to make a guest happy and glad he had come, or miserable and complaining about her service.

"My oper-r-rators shall have zee extra talent," Madame had said decisively in her delightful French accent. "Zay must be efficient. Ah, yes! But zay must also have imagination, poise, an ingr-r-ratiating manner of speech—weez veree be-e-autiful voices. Zay must have *tact*."

Plans for dinner, luncheon, the theatre; for riding, golf, tennis; for swimming, sailing, fishing—all went bounding hither and yon across this board. There were bits of gossip, too, and items of strictly business. Through its copper veins had flowed all the excitement of summer romances at the Seaview Arms for fifteen happy years.

Hundreds of girls had come, worked a while, and gone, during those fifteen years. Each had been personally chosen by Madame DuLhut herself. When Ginger Rogers applied for a position, Madame had instantly pronounced her the ideal type for switchboard operator.

In the first few weeks she had watched Ginger's work closely. Then, to her manager, she had affirmed her first impression.

"Meester Dudley," she had told him emphatically, "a capable night operator eez far more important to us zan a day operator. When zee day ees ovaire, and zee guest eez having—what you call—'let-down' (maybe he ees lonely, maybe he ees hunting somesing else to do for zee evening), he come to zee telephone. A cheery word, a leetle extra care weez heem, make heem veree happy— leeft hees speerits. And at night zere ees more time to do zat." She paused a moment. "Ask our leetle ZheeZhee." She gave Ginger's name its French pronunciation. "Ask *her* eef she would work for us at nights. Geeve her more money, maybe."

It was done.

For the next year and a half Ginger had justified Madame's faith in her. To Mr. Dudley, Madame had said, "Our lettle ZheeZhee ees more zan just zee night operator. She has a mind and she uses eet. Zee guests are cra-a-zy about her. Books, candy, flowers zey send her all zee time."

Mr. Dudley smiled tolerantly. "Well, it's no secret around here that you're pretty crazy about her yourself, Madame," he said.

"Zat I am," Madame replied, quickly. "Eef I could have her for my own child, I should like zat." Madame's smiling old eyes had dimmed at the thought. "You know, Mr. Dudley, I have grandchildren in France—just her age."

Her poor France! Her children and grandchildren! Where were they? What was happening to them since the disasters of war had overcome her native country?

"She feel up a leetle of zat space in *here*," Madame had

added and placed a hand in the region of her heart.

The little telephone room, where Ginger spent most of her waking hours, was as neat and polished, as spick-and-span, as a hospital. It was on the second floor of the Seaview Arms and its one large window, fitted with a draft-glass at the bottom, overlooked the beautiful gardens through a wealth of lacy palms.

On the table, under the window, stood a vase of blood-red roses, their fading loveliness framed in a shaft of soft moonlight. There were dozens of them. Mr. Dunlop, a guest and an old friend of Madame, had sent them to Ginger earlier that evening. Now they filled the little cubicle with a musty, pungent perfume.

There was but one door to the little room and it opened onto a corridor leading to the elevators. Its long pane of translucent glass allowed diffused light to pass through, but objects beyond were only shadows. This door, by the rules of the management, was always locked, for into such sanctums ordinary people may not wander. To have the freedom of such a place, one must know the code, pledge the faith, and, hearing all, tell nothing.

The wall to the right gave the room its importance because that wall held the gigantic switchboard. Four girls by day, and two by night, faced its shining mystery of wires and keys, its plugs and earphones.

These girls talked with kings and rajahs, with bootblacks and barbers, with society women and senators. One had even spoken with President Roosevelt—*"Mr. President? Go ahead, please."*

On this particular evening the eight o'clock rush was nearly over, and Ginger and Patsy were catching their breath. From seven-thirty to eight the board before them bloomed with tiny lights flashing on. Each light was a signal for a call and sometimes there were ten at the same moment, like a flickering Christmas tree. That was the time when dates were arranged, when people were asking, "Are you ready? All right, meet you in the lobby." Or, "Is Joe coming with us? Fine. Come on up." And sometimes that funny one, "Oh, I just can't go. I've got such a headache. The sun, you know." Then a jiggling of the hook, the ringing of another number and, "I got out of it. I can come."

Patsy was thirsty. Detaching her headset from the plug located just above her lap, she went to the water cooler in the corner. With her earphones still on, and the horn-like mouthpiece hung around her neck, she resembled a voodoo princess in full regalia about to invoke her gods.

A lonely light showed on Ginger's board. She plugged in and flicked open her key.

"Operator Seven," she announced.

Instantly her face brightened.

"Oh, Mr. Dunlop, I tried to get you before. I called your house in New York and gave your butler the message. Is he Japanese?"

A gently modulated voice from the other end of the wire, the voice of a man to whom Ginger had talked many times, but whom she had never seen, answered, "Thank you, Ginger, and what did he say?"

"He seemed a bit confused, Mr. Dunlop, and I think perhaps you had better talk to him yourself."

"So?" Mr. Dunlop said the little word with a rising inflection. "What was so confusing about my message, I wonder."

"I told him you said to lay in some sugar because you believed there would be a shortage. What bothered him was how much to get and, since you hadn't told me, I couldn't tell him." This was just before the United States was in the war, and national sugar rationing had not been thought of.

"That was stupid of me, wasn't it?" Mr. Dunlop asked. "I wonder if you would call him again. Just say I think four hundred pounds will be enough. Would you do that for me?"

"Gladly," Ginger answered, then ventured to suggest, "But I could try to get him now and you could talk to him personally. He seems not to understand me very well. He's Japanese, isn't he?"

"He'll understand this time," Mr. Dunlop answered. "I must go out again almost immediately and cannot wait for a long-distance call. Anyway, you do these things very well, Miss Rogers, if you will permit me to say so."

"Thank you," Ginger said. "Shall I try now? It's almost twelve o'clock in New York. Will that be too late?"

"Try it. If my house doesn't answer, then call tomorrow night. There's really no rush."

"Okay, Mr. Dunlop. Thank you."

"The thanks are to you, my dear. Goodnight." Mr.

Dunlop hung up.

Ginger pulled her plug and dialed long distance.

"Dunlop again, huh?" Patsy said. "Acts like he's afraid long distance will bite him. That's the second time this week. What was it last time?"

Ginger gave the number in New York to the long-distance operator before she turned to answer Patsy. "It was his gardener in Miami before. He must have a home there, too."

"Sounds to me like he's trying to make an impression," Patsy sneered. "An apartment in New York, a home in Miami with a garden, four hundred pounds of sugar, and him a bachelor. What's all that about?"

"We're not certain he's a bachelor, Patsy. Remember, we just guessed at that," Ginger said.

"Well, he stays on here month after month and no wife or son or daughter or kith or kin ever calls him up while we're on the board. Seems he won't ever let anybody do anything for him but you. I tried to once, but no soap. He waited until you came on."

Ginger laughed. "That's just because I started with him, I guess. When he first came, I mean."

But Patsy didn't believe it.

"He's *too sweet* for words. I don't like him." She launched into an imitation of Mr. Dunlop. "'Tell my gardener in Miami to move the tree from the front yard to the place in the back yard I pointed out to him last year when I was there!'" The voice and the speech mannerisms were perfect mimicry. "Now, I ask you, what is *that?* A home in Miami and he hasn't been there since last year—still he wants the gardener to move a tree!"

"Well, that's possible," Ginger conceded, despite her amusement.

"Anything's possible in this life, darling," Patsy said. *"But,* when you sit here at a telephone switchboard year after year, your ears get to be eyes and, even if you've never seen 'em, you learn to read people like a book just from hearing their voices and taking their crazy orders. I don't *like* him, I tell you. I don't like the simpering way he calls you every night and asks you all sorts of personal things about yourself."

Ginger smiled tolerantly. "He doesn't mean anything by it. Maybe he's lonely. Anyway he isn't the only one who calls me every night. Why should you dislike him just for that?"

"It isn't 'just for that,'" Patsy shot back. "I just don't like him. Period."

Ginger had only a moment to giggle at the ludicrous firmness of her switchboard partner's hatred of the seemingly harmless Mr. Dunlop. Then her New York call came through and she delivered his message to the Japanese voice that again answered the 'phone. As Mr. Dunlop had predicted, this time he understood and thanked her graciously for the information.

Another light flashed. "Yes, Mr. Bagnall," Ginger said into the mouthpiece that hung about her neck. "You want me to call Mr. Coleman and tell him that you have gone on to the factory and will meet him there at twelve tonight. Right?"

"If you will, Miss Ginger," Mr. Bagnall answered in a well-modulated voice from his suite on the tenth floor. "It will be a big help. I'm in something of a hurry to get away."

"I'll be glad to, Mr. Bagnall, and thank you." She closed her key. Then, as she rang another telephone somewhere in the vast reaches of the hotel, she said to Patsy, "I wonder what Mr. Bagnall looks like. He has such a nice voice."

"He's probably half-past fifty, ugly and beats his children." Patsy was still nettled over the Dunlop matter and couldn't be kind about anyone. "But they all talk to *you* with honey on their tongues. What do you put into that voice that gets 'em?"

Ginger's number answered.

"Mr. Coleman, please," she said. Then, after a short pause, she asked, "Is there anywhere I could reach him right away? The Melody Cocktail Lounge? Thank you." She disconnected and dialed another number.

Patsy said disgustedly, "Bagnall should pay you a secretary's salary."

"Mr. Coleman, please," Ginger answered her call before she answered Patsy. "He's a guest in the lounge. Will you page him? Thank you." Then to Patsy, "Don't forget he sent us a box of candy yesterday."

"He didn't send it to *me*," Patsy rejoined. "And I didn't eat but one piece of it, either. You know candy goes to my hips. But this Bagnall person should get him-

Mr. Bagnall Gave Ginger a Message for Mr. Coleman

self an office and a girl to take care of his business, instead of using a hotel switchboard. And at night, too! Don't the man ever sleep?"

Patsy's pretended bitterness at life and her work was a never-ending source of amusement to Ginger. Patsy was a swell girl, really. There wasn't a service that Ginger did for the guests that Patsy wouldn't do, and didn't do, for them every day. She reserved her gruffness for their private consumption, when they had time to talk, and Ginger was sure that most of this gruffness was put on to relieve the boredom of the long night-shift. She knew that Patsy had a heart as big as a barrel and that, when Patsy answered a call, her voice was sweet and soft and "smiley."

"Mr. Bagnall doesn't sleep much these days, I guess," Ginger answered Patsy. "He's an important designer for Spurlock Aircraft, or something." She was going to add that, in taking care of Mr. Bagnall's business, she felt they were playing their small part in the country's huge war effort. But at that moment Mr. Coleman came to the other end of the line.

"Hullo," he said, shortly.

"Mr. Coleman, this is Operator Seven at the Seaview Arms. Mr. Bagn—"

"Oh, hello, beautiful," Mr. Coleman exclaimed, brightening.

Ignoring the intimate salutation, Ginger went on with her message. When she had finished, and had made him check to be sure he understood, Mr. Coleman wanted to talk more.

"How's about me sending you up something from here?" he asked. "You must be thirsty."

"No, thank you," Ginger answered.

She had always to remember that the hotel guest is always right, and so are all his friends and business associates. But Ginger had learned, through long practice, that even a telephone girl could find protection for her dignity in just the right inflection on a word or the intonation of a phrase. Her "no, thank you" would have been sufficiently definite to anyone in a less playful mood than Mr. Coleman.

"Not even an ice cream soda, a coke or a lollipop?" Coleman persisted. "You can take your choice."

"Not tonight, thank you." Then she said, "It's eleven-ten, Mr. Coleman, and you've only enough time to meet Mr. Bagnall. Could I order a taxi for you?"

Blocked so deftly, Mr. Coleman was sufficiently sophisticated to appreciate it.

"You're a cute little somebody," he said, laughing. "But one of these fine days I'm going to meet you and take that voice out to dinner. See if I don't!"

That's what they all said. Ginger was used to it. In fact, she rarely *heard* it any more and never acknowledged that she had.

"All right," Mr. Coleman went on. "In about ten minutes you can have a taxi for me outside the Melody. Okay?"

"I will," Ginger answered. "Thank you."

Ginger saw that Patsy had been listening, for Patsy's finger flicked a key and there were no calls on her board. It was that hour in the night when calls were few and far between. The board wouldn't pick up again until almost twelve. It was the time of night Patsy always chose for her lectures. Ginger could see the critical look in Patsy's eyes and it made her smile.

"You never let one of 'em get to first base, do you?" Patsy paused for just the right effect. "You're a strange kid! *Weird,* I might add."

Luckily the starter at the motor-court door answered Ginger's ring just then and she could ignore Patsy.

"Send a taxi to the Melody Cocktail Lounge for Mr. Coleman in ten minutes, Joe. He'll be outside waiting. Got it? Okay! Thank you."

But Patsy was not to be diverted. She had things to say and she was going to say them.

Why did Ginger always do it? How did she have the heart? She was pretty, almost beautiful. She could have her pick of the lot. But what did she do? She squelched 'em, that's what!

Amused, Ginger glanced in Patsy's direction.

"You're getting your wires crossed, honey," she said. "A while ago you were mad because a man was too sweet to me, and now you're mad because—"

Patsy was being half in fun and all in earnest. Almost two years of long nights at this switchboard together had brought to these two girls a complete understanding, a fine friendship.

"You know what I mean and don't pretend you don't. There are several nice men in this hotel. Oh, I know the rules say we are not to go out with the guests, but you make a religion of not doing it."

Ginger smiled. "I notice you never go out when you're asked, either."

"What do you mean, when *I'm* asked?" Patsy wanted to know. "Nobody ever asks *me* and you know it. I'm too wide and too short. They forgot to give me a nose and my second chin's got more character than my first one. I'm pigeon-toed and my underskirt's always hanging and there's nothing I can do about it."

As Ginger's merry laugh rang out through the little room, Patsy added, "And the name's *Patsy Potts!* Remember?"

Dear, comical Patsy. You laughed *with* her not *at* her. She didn't really look as bad as she painted herself. That was why it was always funny when she picked herself to pieces for the entertainment of her friends. Patsy wasn't really "too wide and too short." She was just plump, in spots. "Yeah, all the wrong spots," Patsy would say. Her underskirt didn't *always* hang down, just at times, and usually when Patsy was trying to make a good impression. Patsy was pretty when she "fixed herself up." But, best of all to Ginger, Patsy was a true-blue friend. She was devoted to Ginger—all her dreams of romance hovered about the head of her friend, rather than about her own.

"Laugh if you want to," Patsy went on. "But you get

the chances any girl would give her right eye for. And what do you do with them? You spend your time on that silly Jim Daley."

On the subject of Jim Daley, Patsy could be vitriolic. "A high-school romance!" she would scoff. "Kid stuff! And you'll probably marry the jerk and waste all your beauty on the desert air, or something. I only wish *I* were in your shoes. I'd show you!"

But a light had flashed on Patsy's board and Ginger was spared the oft-repeated catalogue of the things Patsy would do—if she could be Ginger for just a little while.

Like an actress stepping onto the stage, Patsy's whole manner changed. Her voice moved up into sweetness and smiles, as she said, "Seaview Arms. Good evening!"

Then, as she listened, her eyebrows lifted and she looked toward Ginger, who was watching her.

"Miss Joyce Grantland?" she asked. "Who's calling, please?"

By the tone of her voice Ginger could tell that Patsy already knew who was calling.

"Mr. Gregg Phillips?" Patsy asked meaningly, thus getting the information over to Ginger. "Just a moment, please."

She closed her key and, as she rang the Grantland suite on the sixth floor, she said, "There! That's your barefoot millionaire calling another girl. Y'see what happens!"

Miss Grantland answered.

"Mr. Phillips calling, Miss Grantland. Go ahead please." Patsy closed her key, then glanced sidewise at Ginger to see how the information had affected her.

But Ginger was smiling with not a trace of concern. Patsy sniffed in disgust. Then the light flashed on Patsy's board, indicating the Phillips-Grantland conversation was at an end. Patsy pulled the plugs.

A light glowed on Ginger's board. It was a call from outside.

She answered, "Seaview Arms. Good evening."

Gregg Phillips' voice said, "Well, that's better. Why didn't you answer when I called a moment ago?"

"Because your call didn't come in on my board," Ginger answered, mildly amused.

"What do you mean, allowing me to wander around over strange people's switchboards?"

Ginger liked Gregg Phillips when he talked this way.

"Oh, you were doing all right," she answered.

"That's the way to talk," Gregg came back. "I always like my girl friends to be just a little jealous. Puts spice into romance. Look, Operator Seven, when am I going to see you? Will it be in this life or do I have to wait for my next incarnation?"

Ginger laughed.

"No can do, sir," she answered. "Rules and regulations of the Seaview Arms."

"Then I'll move out of the darned old place," he countered. "Couldn't do it in a better cause."

"And I'd get fired in the same cause," Ginger replied.

"Say, what is this?" Gregg asked. "The run-around? You don't if I do and you don't if I do! Know what *I* think? I think you're making the whole thing up just to keep me interested. Well, all right, I'm interested. Now how's about me coming up to see you, say in about fifteen minutes? I'm not at the hotel now, but I can get there awful fast."

"Ughuh!" Ginger grunted, playfully.

She couldn't be conventional with Gregg (she was beginning to think of him by his first name). She liked these regular evening calls. They thrilled her more than she would ever have admitted even to herself.

"You couldn't get in even if you did come up," she said.

"You mean they lock you into that torture chamber?" Gregg pretended to be horrified. "Well, it's not such a bad idea, at that. Still and all, young woman, you could do worse than have a date with me."

"Could I?" Ginger teased.

"Now don't you get smart with me!" Gregg replied. "You know very well you like to have me calling you up, and I know you'd like to go out with me. A-n-d, one of these days, when I'm not too busy, I'm going to think up some way to get you to do it. In the meantime, though, you'll have to possess your soul in patience. Good night, Seven."

"Goodnight, Mr. Phillips," Ginger laid stress on the pronunciation of his last name.

"The name's *Gregg*," he said.

"Yes, Mr. Phillips," Ginger replied.

"Oh, you're *im*-possible!" His gruffness was part of the game they played. "Good NIGHT!" And he hung up.

Ginger laughed as she disconnected.

Patsy, watching her face, saw the momentary, fleeting, faraway look that nestled in Ginger's deep blue eyes. A smile played about the soft lips making little dimples scurry here and there. Patsy's romantic heart for a moment knew satisfaction. Now here was something, she was thinking, that could be extremely worth while. *"Imagine Ginger married to all that money!"* she said to herself.

Aloud, Patsy observed, "Well, that leaves only Miles Harrington. He hasn't checked in yet this evening." Then when a light suddenly appeared on Ginger's board, she added, "Speaking of the devil, you hear the flutter of his wings. There's Miles. Wanta bet?"

But Ginger was saying, "Operator Seven . . . Yes, Mr. Dunlop."

Patsy muttered disgustedly under her breath, "What, *him* again?"

Ginger told Mr. Dunlop the results of her talk with his servant in New York.

"I'm beginning to see, Miss Rogers," he said, "that if one wants a thing well done, one gives it to you to do."

"Service is our motto, Mr. Dunlop," Ginger replied quickly.

"I know that," he answered. "But you distill it to such a high degree of refinement."

Ginger saw that Patsy had her key open and that Patsy was making faces.

"Goodnight," Ginger said and disconnected.

Patsy, the imitator, was off again. "The inslings and the impercipities of man have flown to such a high flanatus. Where does that guy get that stuff? Geeee! But *how* I don't like him."

CHAPTER TWO

Something happened the very next day that changed the whole life of Ginger Rogers. It was also destined to change the lives of all Americans, of Englishmen, of Australians, of South Americans—and of all of the inhabitants of the *civilized* world!

Japan treacherously attacked Pearl Harbor while her envoys were talking peace in Washington!

As one person, the people of the United States jumped to their feet, their mouths wide open in horror. Nobody doubted what their next reaction would be. Like a whirlwind gathering momentum as it swept forward, the United States moved from defense to offense. The American people, disorganized and bickering over the question of war, solidified, unified and cooperated with each other.

In aircraft factories not ten miles from the luxurious Seaview Arms new and deadly weapons—secret weapons —were soon in the process of manufacture. There was a new bomb-sight, its accuracy the truest of any yet devised by man. There was a plane, its speed far outstripping anything owned by any other country in the world. There was a gun for the plane's forward cockpit that swung in any direction and wreaked devastation on anything that came under its aim.

As though to exemplify the manner in which America could rise from deep slumber and land on her feet with both fists flying, Madame DuLhut was among the first to come out of her shock and go into action. She called her staff into the office which she shared with Mr. Dudley, her manager.

"My friends," she said as she rose and stood before them, her black eyes aflame with patriotic zeal, "in a few hours America weel be at war. My beloved France fell before zee enemy weez hardly a struggle. Zee horror of zee attack paralyzed her. My people, zey could not believe. Zey did nossing! Zat must not happen here!"

Catching the fervor of her spirit, her staff applauded.

"Eet weel be entirely up to you and me, indiveedually, zat dees does not happen here! Are you going to let eet?"

Cries of "No! No! No!" came from the faces turned up to her.

"Zen, our duty ees clear." Suddenly she was the military general planning the attack. "We have a beeg hotel here. I say, 'we,' because to me eet eez beeg and fine because *you* have helped me make eet so. Your faithfulness, energy and good work make eet so. For year on year we have served zee happy vacationer from all ovaire zee world. We make heem more happy. Now we weel ask heem to leave us."

The expressions of the faces before her asked one question. Was Madame going to close the hotel?

Madame answered it:

"We are going to ask heem to leave us and we are go-

Madame DuLhut Called Her Staff Together

ing to eenvite zat horde of aircraft workers who weel come and weel find no ozzer place to leeve. We weel ask zem to come to our hotel to leeve."

The staff rose in instant enthusiasm. Each one applauded in his own way.

"Bravo! Bravo!" came from the throat of Giuseppe, the Italian maitre-d'hotel.

"Magnifique!" exclaimed Gaston, the French chef, with emphatic gestures.

"Vonderful!" cried Adolph, the German pastry cook.

"That's fine!"—"Hurray!"—"A swell idea!"—were the words of the Americans who were born here. But they were no more enthusiastic than those others who were America's adopted children.

Pleased at the whole-hearted reception of her plan, Madame continued, "Eet weel mean change. We must lower zee rates. We weel feel up zee rooms weez beds, one bed more, two beds, three beds. Eet weel maybe not be so good *for* our fine tapestries, our furniture, but—," and she smiled encouragingly—"but zay could not go in a—what you say?—holier cause. Zen, my friends, eet ees done."

The next morning all the hotel's guests received letters asking them to relinquish their rooms. At her desk bright and early, Madame received her guests, making lists of the earliest date each one could arrange to go, laughing with them as each in turn gladly consented to go and thus do his bit for the "cause." But when Mr. Dunlop entered her office Madame met her first dissenter.

"Now, Zabel," she said, with a cajoling smile, "don't be a leetle boy."

"But where can I go, Millinet?" he asked, pouting. "This has been like home to me."

"Home? Zat ees funny, coming from you, Zabel, you, who travel zee whole wide world and nevaire stop."

"But you are being so precipitate, my dear. I could not find a place to live so hurriedly. Why must *you* be so patriotically concerned, Millinet?" Mr. Dunlop argued.

"You do not surprise me, Zabel. A bachelor he ees always zee selfish man of zee world. You have no home, so you have no country. You are decadent, Zabel, deteriorated." She shrugged her expressive shoulders, but smiled as she spoke. "Do you not theenk to yourself of the meaning, eef thees country, too, fall under zee cruel Nazi heel? You had to leave France because of eet. You told me zat, yourself. Zees time you must stay and push your shoulder to zee wheel." Then she ended playfully, "Now, get out of my hotel, you bad friend, and let me have zee suite for zee leetle working boys. Go! Go! *Go!*"

Madame could hardly forbear laughing outright at the discomfort she was causing the immaculate little man, who sat on the very edge of his chair before her desk, his white brow furrowed in a petulant pucker. Always touched by the weakness of her fellow creatures, Madame made a clicking little sound with her tongue, "Eet ees so veree too bad," she said. "I fear me you are going to weep, Zabel." Then she thought of something. "Well, eef you must have a leetle more time, zen you may move into the bungalow in zee yard. Eet weel be very expensive for just you alone, for you weel have to pay me zee usual rates."

Mr. Dunlop's face came out from behind its dark cloud. "If I could only stay a week or two more!"

He seemed overcome with joy. It was as if all the grave problems of a lifetime were now settled for him.

"But, you can have zee bungalow only until I am full up here," Madame said, quickly and definitely. "Zen you weel have to go. I weel need eet, too, for my aircraft workers."

Mr. Dunlop's acceptance was a hasty retreat, before Madame could change her mind. He hardly stopped to thank her for the reprieve. Madame shook her head, puzzled, as he closed the door behind him, but she hadn't time to give the matter further thought, for other guests were waiting their turns to talk with her, ready to give up their winter vacations and go their various ways.

That evening, sitting on a lawn seat conveniently hidden from view by a crowded growth of bushes, Zabel Dunlop saw a girl hurrying up the walk to the main entrance of the hotel. Young, slender and shapely, her long legs carried her with a rhythmic swing that started at her waistline and ended in firm, athletic footfalls.

As he watched, he suddenly realized that here was the little star of the Seaview Arms switchboard.

A mischievous wind caught the brim of her wide leghorn hat and slapped it hard against her face. It rippled the soft folds of her dress. She made a whirling about-face to keep the dust from blowing into her eyes.

A great orange sun was drowning itself at sunset in a purple haze. Dangling from the high arc of heaven, a silver moon was growing bolder by the minute. The very atmosphere was charged with color.

The girl stopped and stood, just looking. And, as though to entice her to remain, soft music floated on the wind from the dining patio of the hotel. Dunlop watched, fascinated. To him the girl was like a wind-blown fairy, poised to take flight.

In the southern sky a tulle cloud was changing from pink to lavender to blue as it wafted back, losing itself in the deepening mist of the approaching California night. The girl smiled up at it, wholly unaware of watching eyes.

Then she sighed. That sigh was saying, "Flower-studded gardens, darkening trees, skimming gulls, sweet salt air and my favorite time of day, my favorite time of year. And I must go in and leave it all."

She took a long breath and began walking backward, slowly.

Zabel Dunlop thought it a little tragic that this girl, loving the outdoors and made for it, must, so early in the evening, climb upon a high stool, face a black switch-board and begin the manipulation of plugs and wires and keys which would connect people, who wanted to talk, with other people, whether they wanted to listen or not. He wondered if, perhaps, she were a little tired of it all.

To the six-hundred-odd guests of the Seaview Arms

she must be courteous and kind, no matter how she felt, no matter what they might say or do. When she passed down this walk again, it would be three o'clock in the morning. The sun and the moon, both, would be gone and she would be wending a weary way homeward in that darkest hour before the dawn. Dunlop wondered if such a girl might not welcome some way to be free of that humdrum routine of life.

In his imagination he followed the rest of her day. At the corner she probably waited for a bus each morning, one that stopped somewhere near her home. No doubt, her mother would time her sleep to awaken just then, rise on an elbow to look out of the window, or come to the door as her daughter walked the few steps that led up to the house, alone.

He visualized the girl, unlocking the door and softly creeping in. In the kitchen, no doubt, there would be a bottle of milk on the table, a sandwich or a piece of cake. The evening paper would be there, too. She would munch and read. Maybe she would walk about the house awhile, noiselessly, then creep to bed. And, when she awoke to-morrow, the sun would be sliding down the western sky again. What a dreary life for a vital, young girl! Wouldn't almost anyone do *anything* to get away from that?

Then it happened!

The girl stumbled over a crack in the walk. Her purse went one way, spilling out all its little vanities. Her hat, caught upon a gust of wind, planted itself firmly, like a great white flower, in the top of an oleander bush.

Zabel Dunlop jumped up to help. She saw him.

"I—I—beg your pardon," she said in her confusion, while, with both hands, she struggled to hold together a luxury of dark brown hair, which had been so neatly turned in a page-boy bob.

Now, with copper lights glistening as it danced, her hair became part of the sunset caught just above her blue eyes.

"Lovelier than I thought." Dunlop was saying to himself, as, aloud, he mumbled, "It's quite all right."

He picked up her scattered belongings, then jumped and rescued the leghorn hat. He handed them to her with a polite bow.

"Thank you very much," she said with some return of composure. "I shouldn't have stopped, I guess."

"But the evening was so extraordinarily lovely." He was smiling discreetly. "You couldn't very well be blamed for that."

He saw a fleeting sign of recognition of his voice pass across her eyes.

For a moment it seemed as if she were going to ignore it. Then very frankly she said, "You're Mr. Dunlop."

"That is right," he said, bowing again. "And you are Ginger Rogers."

"Well," she smiled, showing fine white teeth, "this is a case of two voices suddenly materializing and becoming people. May I thank you personally, Mr. Dunlop, for all the nice flowers and things you send to Patsy and me?"

"You may," he answered. "But it isn't at all necessary.

You always earn them. You're a very efficient and obliging young woman."

"Thank you."

He could see that she wanted to get away as quickly, though politely, as she could.

"It has been nice to meet you, Mr. Dunlop. And now I must hurry—I'm sure I'm late. Good day."

"It's been most pleasant," Dunlop said, bowing again. "Good day."

"So that was Ginger Rogers," Zabel Dunlop was saying to himself when he heard a voice coming from behind him.

He turned. A yellow roadster had pulled up to the curb and stopped.

"Miss Rogers," the voice was calling. "Hey! Ginger!"

Dunlop watched Ginger as she turned. She saw that it was Gregg Phillips' long, flannel-clad legs emerging over the low door of the car and, without a word or a backward glance, she fled into the hotel entrance.

Gregg called again, "Hey, Ginger, wait for baby." But Ginger was gone.

The scene pleased Dunlop. For years he had been seeing Gregg Phillips in one part of the world or another, always followed about from place to place by rich girls, poor girls, shop girls. Once, in Paris, there had been a Princess of the royal blood! But Gregg had always managed to dodge them all. Now he was being dodged, and by a little telephone operator!

That night, when Zabel Dunlop called Ginger, accord-

Ginger Fled into the Hotel Entrance

ing to his usual custom, he felt that she seemed to be embarrassed by the thought that they had met. While he was speaking about something, not too important, she excused herself. When she came back on again she said:

"I have another call, Mr. Dunlop. So I shall have to say 'Goodnight.' "

"That will be Miles Harrington," Dunlop thought.

It was.

"Here I am, Miles," Ginger spoke into the telephone.

"Good," Miles replied. "Look, Ginger, I have tickets for the opening of a picture at Grauman's. It's Friday night, your night off. How's about it?"

"Sounds fine," Ginger answered. "I'd love to go."

"Then it's a date. I'll call your house Friday afternoon and we'll fix up the time and such."

"Good."

"And we'll go dancing after. So tell your Mommie you might be late getting home." Miles seemed to be in a hurry.

"She won't mind that," Ginger answered. "It's a date."

"Check?"

"Check!"

He hung up.

"Now that's something like it," Patsy could hardly contain herself. "Those aircraft workers make good money. He'll take you to swell places, I bet. Maybe to Ciro's or somewhere like that." Patsy's eyes sparkled. "Those foreigners are real gentlemen, too, aren't they? They bring you flowers and kiss your hand and treat you like a lady, don't they?"

"Patsy, you're an incurable romantic!" Ginger laughed, adding, "I got those words out of a book."

"Oh, gee!" Patsy thrilled. "I wish it was my day off, too, so I could be at your house when you two leave for the show. Him tall and dark and handsome, looking down at you. He *is* handsome, isn't he?"

"Oh, he's nice looking," Ginger smiled. "But he's not so awfully tall. A little taller than I, maybe."

That robbed Patsy of a part of her romance, but not too much. "Well, anyway, you'll both be in evening clothes and you'll step into his limousine and—"

Ginger laughed outright at that. "Stop it, Patsy!"

At that moment a light came up on Ginger's board. It was the front office.

When Ginger answered, Madame's kind voice said, "ZheeZhee, weel you come to me down to my office for a leetle while? Patsy can handle zee board. Yes?"

"Oh, yes, Madame," Ginger answered, overjoyed.

These little visits which she was privileged to have with Madame from time to time were rare treats to her. This older, wiser woman, whose richer, fuller life she so admired, never failed to give Ginger some of her wisdom to take away with her. On such occasions Ginger made herself a sponge, drawing in all that Madame said and did. Later she digested it and made it her own.

Carefully Ginger took the headpiece from across her hair, laid it on the board in front of her. Motioning Patsy to take over, she dashed out of the room, down the corridor and, instead of waiting for an elevator, walked down the stairway beside the shaft.

If she hurried now she could take her time going through the lobby.

CHAPTER THREE

THE SCARLET CLOAK

A broad staircase led from the mezzanine floor downward into the heart of a spacious lobby. Ginger always paused at the top of those stairs whenever she came that way. She loved the costly setting with its high-backed chairs, its clusters of palms, its Spanish arches and great beams.

In the middle of an expanse of tiled floor, a fountain bubbled over a blue marble globe, the crystal-clear water splashing into a basin filled with rocks and fern, lilies and goldfish. Standing there, Ginger could feel the grandeur and the glamour of it all.

Ladies in evening gowns of every hue of the rainbow and men in the formal black of dinner clothes strolled over the deep carpet or stood in groups, talking. Diamonds flashed from hair and hand and dress. Laughter and a pleasant hum of modulated voices floated up to Ginger. A telephone bell jangled from the desk of the clerk.

A young man in sweat-shirt and tennis shoes strode in from the motor court and up to the elevator with such speed that Ginger felt he must go right on through the heavy steel gate. He stopped short, then stood waiting. Someone late for a dinner appointment, she thought. He would probably rush into his room, pick up the telephone, jiggle the hook impatiently and order something rushed to him "right away."

Her elastic mind delighted in imagining the drama of this busy hotel. People, wholly unrelated to each other, elbowing each other in corridors and elevators, eating in the same dining rooms, playing on the same beaches, sunning in the same gardens. She knew, as no one else in the hotel knew, that these people rarely made friends among themselves. The telephone switchboard told her that.

Standing at the top of the stairway, looking down at the picture below, the life of a great hotel spread before her in a completed pattern. She had never visited a guest room or suite, except Madame's penthouse on the roof, but she could reach them all through the magic of her switchboard; and her imagination told her how they must look.

With her hand on the rail, Ginger began her descent of the carpeted stairway. In her dark dress, with its white collar and cuffs, she was in pointed contrast to the colorful scene in the lobby. Many standing about turned to look as she passed. She made her way directly, by the shortest route, to the door marked, "Manager."

A hand closed gently over her forearm. Gregg Phillips had come across the lobby and overtaken her. She had not seen him before. Now she looked up into his smiling, hazel eyes. How handsome he was in evening clothes! She noticed that his blond hair, cut short and brushed back in an effort to control its natural wave, was even more ashen against the black and white of his formal attire.

"Hey, Seven!" he said. "What are you doing off the preserve tonight?"

"Going to the office."

He had thoughtfully relinquished her arm. She liked that.

"Getting fired, I hope."

Ginger laughed. "I don't think so, but you never can tell. I could get fired for this, you know."

Gregg looked about the room, "Where is that manager? Why is he never around at times like this? Why does Madame pay him a salary, unless it's to watch out for things and enforce the rules?"

"You're crazy!" Ginger turned to leave. "Madame is waiting for me in the office. I've got to get in there. Have a good time, wherever you're going."

He walked beside her. "Just to a concert in town. Wish you were going along."

Involuntarily she looked back over her shoulder to see with whom he might be going. Gregg saw her interest and found it gave him a small sense of triumph.

"I'm taking the Grantlands," he exclaimed. "Mother and daughter."

"That's nice." The little barb she put into the two words made Gregg chuckle inwardly.

They were at the door of the office. Ginger had a hand on the knob. And, as though to make the most of a meeting that would not be repeated soon again, Gregg grew more serious.

"You know I'd rather it were with you, don't you?" he said.

"Well, I—I—" His sudden sincerity confused her.

"You do. And believe it, Ginger, because it's true."

Longer than they knew, they stood there looking into each other's eyes. Yes, she believed it! Ginger turned the knob. The door opened. She stepped inside and slowly closed the door. That picture of him, standing there, filling the doorway with his tall, young frame, looking down at her with his sincere hazel eyes, would not leave her for several days to come. She stood for a moment on the other side of the door. Her heart was beating with an unfamiliar swiftness. Then she turned and opened the door to Madame's private office.

Madame DuLhut rose from her chair behind the desk and came to meet Ginger. Taking both the girl's hands in her own, Madame looked at her, seeing the unusual pinkness of her cheeks and feeling the slight trembling of her hands.

"You deed not need to hurry so." Madame's humorous old eyes were filled with her fondness for Ginger. "Yet zat peenk in your cheek ees very becoming."

"You are looking very lovely yourself, Madame," Ginger said as she touched the softness of Madame's lavender evening gown, grateful that Madame could not guess the true source of the pink in her cheek.

"ZheeZhee, I have not seen you for days."

Madame guided Ginger to a chair and selected the

love seat opposite for herself. On her shoulder was a
splash of pink camillias, fastened with a diamond pin.

As Madame turned and kicked the train of her evening
gown behind her, Ginger thought again, as she had so
many times before when watching Madame, that only a
Frenchwoman knows how to wear clothes, what to wear
with them, and how to handle them. Everything Madame
DuLhut wore looked stunning and right. Her accessories
were always correctly simple. Ginger mentally made a
note of this rule of Madame's smartness to use for herself and her own clothes.

"That is *such* a beautiful gown!" Ginger exclaimed, as
she watched it fall into graceful folds when Madame sank
to the chair.

Without touching the dress, or seeming to be aware
of it, the Frenchwoman had made it obey her. Now, as
she sat there, she might have been posing for a picture.

Madame was not unaware of her young friend's interest. The hungry eyes of the girl, reaching out for in-
struction and believing Madame to be an inspired ex-
ample, warmed the older woman's heart.

"Eet ees nice, eesn't it?" Madame answered simply.

Ginger liked this frank appreciation. This, too, she
tagged for her own use.

Why shouldn't one think one's own clothes nice? You
bought a dress because you liked it, and wore it because
you thought it suited you. Then why pretend you thought
it "just an old thing I whipped up out of a lamp shade,"
or something equally silly? You like it so you say so, if

you are called upon to say anything.

Then Madame was asking, "ZheeZhee, you have heard what I am doing—about zee hotel?"

"You mean, opening it to the aircraft workers? Oh, yes, and I think it is wonderful! So does everyone."

"Zee hotel weel not be the same any more, ZheeZhee," Madame said. "And eet weel mean a veree much change for you. We weel be busier, and zee spirit of zee hotel weel —weel be—"

"I know what you mean, Madame," Ginger hastened to supply what Madame seemed hesitant about saying. "It will mean that the playtime is over. I shall be just the commercial telephone operator. Isn't that it?"

"Yes, eet ees, and I am sorry, veree sorry. We had zee great fun, deedn't we? And I do not want you to forget how to be zee special night operator, because, someday, all zees weel be ovaire and we weel be returning to our old ways again. But by zen maybe you weel—well, anyway, I hope you weel stay on weez us, but—"

"Stay on with you! You mean, you thought I might want to leave the hotel? Why, Madame, of course I want to stay on. I want to help, too." Then quickly she added, "And, since you are cutting your prices, you may return me to the salary of the regular commercial operator. It wouldn't be fair to—"

"We shall see, we shall see about zat," Madame broke in. "We shall see how eet turns out. You don't know, I don't know, what eet weel be like. We weel wait for zat to happen. In zee meantime, I have somesing else to

talk to you about. Gregg Phillips came to me zees afternoon . . . ."

"Oh, he *didn't!*" Ginger couldn't believe it.

The pink returned to her cheeks—Madame saw that.

"Ah, zen you know. Oh, how nice. Leesin, my child;
he ees a veree nice boy. He ees a very sane young man.
He like you. Ah, I see you know he does." Madame was
enjoying this vision of young love. "I have told heem eet
ees all right weez me eef he take you out some nice place
to dance, maybe."

Ginger was blushing.

"Oh, Madame, I . . . Well, that is very nice of you to
break your rules for me. But I don't know what to say.
I couldn't go, anyway. Mother wouldn't allow me to.
She has some very definite ideas about working girls going out with rich young men."

Madame was surprised, even a little shocked.

"What you mean? She weel not let you go just because
the young man ees reech? Why ees zat? She do not want
you to marry a man weez money?"

Ginger sprang quickly to her mother's defense. "Oh,
no, it isn't that. Mother feels the rich young men do not
want to marry working girls. She's probably right."

"Your Mama eez Puritan, or old-fashion' maybe? She
want you only to go weez zee man you are going to marry?" Madame asked.

"No, it isn't that. She let me go with Miles Harrington.
He seems to have more money than anyone I've ever
gone out with. It's just—"

"Who ees Miles Harrington?" Madame's question held a startling amount of concern in it.

"A young man I met at a party. Somebody introduced him to me. I forget just who now. One of my friends, though. He's rather nice looking and takes me to openings. I'm going to an opening with him on Friday night."

Ginger found, in telling Madame, that she, herself, knew very little about Miles Harrington.

"What ees eet when your Mama weel permit you to go weez a man she just meets and weel not let you go weez a man whose family zee whole world knows all about?"

"Well, it does sound funny when you put it like that." Ginger was a little apologetic for her mother's stern views on such subjects. "But Mother will not allow me to have even one date with Gregg, I know; so she will never have a chance of meeting him, or learning how nice he really is."

"Oh, zat ees such a pitee." Sometimes Madame could not understand the "rules" of American mothers. "Such a great pitee. But maybe eet weel all come about some day, yes?" Then she shrugged her shoulders, as only a Frenchwoman knows how to do it, putting an end to the topic with, "But mamas always know zee best way. And now I tell you what I brought you down here for. See zat."

Madame pointed to a box on her desk. Ginger had been so interested she had not noticed it before. It was so large that it covered almost the entire top. It was a white suit box, tied with a great scarlet bow of wide

"Eet Ees for You," Madame Said

ribbon, and attached to the ribbon was a tag. It looked like something you received at Christmas.

Madame rose and started toward it. Ginger followed her. Madame put her fingers under the great bow and held it out to Ginger.

"Eet ees for you," she said.

Ginger's eyes grew wide with wonder and surprise. She took the box from Madame's hands and rested it on the edge of the desk. She glanced at the tag. "Ginger Rogers, Seaview Arms Hotel," was typed on it.

Slowly she took the ends of the bow in her two hands and pulled. It untied easily. Madame brushed the ribbon from the box and Ginger lifted the lid. Her eyes were dancing in happy anticipation as she looked at Madame.

Then, as though wishing to keep the surprise for herself as long as she could, she began to unfold, one by one, the white tissue sheets. Something glowed through the sheerness of the paper like the sultry embers on a dying hearth.

There it was!

"Oh, how beautiful!" Madame exclaimed.

Ginger's lips shaped a silent "Oh!"

"Eet ees a coat! A scarlet coat!" Madame cried.

Ginger's fingers roamed caressingly over the fineness of the coat's texture. She lifted it. A soft, self-colored hood, fastened behind the exquisitely designed collar, dropped down the back.

The two women looked at each other in surprise. Then Madame exclaimed, as she gathered the folds from the box and let them fall toward the floor, "Eet eesn't a coat. Eet has no sleeves! Eet ees a *cloak!* A scarlet opera cloak!"

"A—scarlet—opera—cloak—for me?" The words were both exclamation and question.

"But, Madame, you shouldn't have, really you shouldn't!"

It was Madame's turn to be surprised.

"But I deedn't, my child. Somebody sent eet. I do not know. Zere ees a card, maybe." She began fumbling in the box for it.

They both hunted. They took each sheet of tissue apart from the others. There was no card. There was no trace of the identity of the sender.

A sudden thought took the wonder out of Ginger's eyes and replaced it with apprehension.

"Madame, you don't suppose it was—?"

"Gregg Phillips? Of course not!" Madame was definite. "Gregg would have much better taste zan zees. I mean, he would not send a girl a cloak."

Relieved, and once more filled with admiration for the mysterious scarlet cloak, Ginger put it to her face and slyly peered into the long mirror that hung on the opposite wall of Madame's office.

Madame, watching, saw the femininity of the gesture and, joining in the spirit of a young girl with something new and elegant to wear, said, "Eet ees just zee right color for you, ZheeZhee. Here, put eet on."

She took the cloak and, shaking it out, draped it about

Ginger's shoulders with a gentle pat here and there. Then she stood away to get the effect. Madame was pleased with what she saw.

Ginger walked toward the mirror. The long, full folds of scarlet moved with her and billowed back from the broad shoulders with the grace of an ostrich plume in the movements of the fandango. The girl walking toward her in the mirror was someone whom Ginger had never seen before, someone smart, chic, and styled by a French couturiere. Her chin went up and her shoulders came slightly forward. Yes, that would be the way to carry so wonderful a wrap. She had borrowed the gesture from Madame without knowing it.

Then, in sudden girlish disappointment, she turned back. "But, Madame, I can't keep it. I'll have to send it back."

"But zere ees nowhere to send eet back," Madame shrugged. "ZheeZhee, you are, what you call, 'stuck weez eet!' "

CHAPTER FOUR

THE SLEIGHT-OF-HAND INCIDENT

Ginger was standing before the mirror in her ging-ham-clad bedroom, brushing her hair, when Mary Rogers called from the kitchen, "Ginger, Jimmy is here."

Continuing her whispered counting mentally, *"Thirty-one, thirty-two, thirty-three,"* Ginger answered, "All right, Mother, I'll be there in a little while."

Her hair had to have a hundred strokes of the brush each day to keep it shiny and lustrous. With head bent forward she brought the brush up from the nape of her neck in long and heavy sweeps.

There was never anything exciting in Jimmy Daley's frequent calls. Living just around the corner in a little cottage very like their own, he had only to leap the back fence, come down the alley, in at their back gate and into the kitchen. Jimmy seemed to enjoy a visit with Mary as much as he did with her. He came over many times when he knew she wouldn't be there. So why hurry?

"Forty-eight, forty-nine . . . ." Her arm needed rest.

She straightened. A scarlet reflection in the mirror, coming through the closet door, brought her eyes about. A smile crossed her face. There it was! The scarlet cloak. You couldn't hide it even in a closet. What a splash of color it was among her other things! It made them all look somber and dull.

She crossed the room and entered the closet. Her black lace evening gown hung beside the cloak. She took it down and, draping the cloak over the shoulders of the gown, held both up to her chin before the mirror. Then she sighed. If she could only wear them together to-night! Miles Harrington would know how to appreciate that cloak. Everyone wore such beautiful clothes to premières, and with this cloak, she would be as well turned out as any of them.

Her smile faded as she remembered the talk which she had had with her mother that morning. She retraced her steps and hooked the hanger over the top of the closet door. She picked up the brush. Now where was she? Oh, yes, *"Fifty, fifty-one . . . ."*

She had no fault to find with Mary because of her de-cision. Receiving a garment like that, out of the blue, well, it was unusual, to say the least. She, herself, hadn't been able to make up her mind what to do about it. Of course Mary was right! A girl couldn't wear clothing some anon-ymous person had sent her!

Yet, that look on Mary's face had been *fear!* What was Mary afraid of? Thinking back, she remembered that that expression of fear had been deepening in her moth-er's eyes for the past year. It had something to do with her being out in the world, earning her living. Now Gin-ger was having experiences apart from her mother. Mary would always hate the fate that had robbed her child of her proper girlhood in the protection of a home and family. She would always be afraid that no good could come of it.

What a "brick" Mother had been through all these years! It seemed that she was always trying, in an almost tragic way, to make up to Ginger for something which she had lost. But how could you lose what you'd never had? How could you miss what you'd never known?

Ginger could remember the long-ago time, when they had first found themselves alone. As young as she was, somehow she had known the struggle which Mary had had, unprepared and unfitted as she had been to meet such an emergency. Yet her mother had set her thin, little lips and, by some miracle of God's own grace, had held them together and kept them going. Day by day the manna had fallen. They had had a wonderful life together, really. Ginger's heart was full of gratitude for all their blessings and she wondered if it would not be wise to have a heart-to-heart talk with her little mother. Perhaps, by recounting those blessings, one by one, she might bring peace to Mary's burdened heart.

Could it be that her mother did not trust her? Or was it that mothers never knew when their daughters had grown up? There was the matter of this cloak, for instance. But, no, that was too far-fetched to be held as a criterion. Any mother would show anxiety over such a thing.

But Gregg! That was different. As Madame DuLhut had said, his family history was an open book for the whole world to read. It was a simple "boy meets girl" story which she had related to her mother. It was unreasonable that his having wealth, a fact for which he was not accountable, could make him an undesirable friend. Yes, Mary had been unreasonable. She had, for the first time, put her foot down and demanded a promise of Ginger that she would never see him or go out with him. It was strange! Gregg was really the nicest boy she had ever met. It was all pretty puzzling.

"*Ninety-seven, ninety-eight, ninety-nine, one hundred.* That's done."

She put down the brush and turned around. The scarlet cloak filled her eyes with its dash and beauty.

"Now what am I going to do about *you?*" she asked it.

Patsy had said, "There's nothing to it. I'd wear it, if it had been sent to me, you can bet."

Under Patsy's influence it had seemed so easy and right to accept it and wear it. She had probably brought that feeling home with her when she had shown the cloak to Mary, her mother.

"We'll just dye you a pretty, warm brown and you'll make a very fittin' cover for the parlor sofie," she said to the cloak.

Laughing to herself, she tied a blue ribbon about her head and, humming, went out toward the kitchen.

She pushed open the swinging door. "Hi, Jimmy, 'ol fellow." She looked where she thought Jimmy would be. "Well, where are you?"

From the floor came Jimmy's muffled voice. "I'm

down under, pal. How are you, and how's the weather up there?"

As he spoke he pulled his head from under the sink and Ginger saw that he had a wrench in his hand. He had been tightening the plumbing, probably by prearrangement with Mary, because he had on a pair of coveralls. His hair was tousled, his hands were grimy, but his eyes were dancing. Jimmy was always happy when he was doing something for somebody.

And this was the boy of Mary's choice for her.

"We know his family and they all like us," Mary had said. "It's those things that make for happiness in marriage. He's a good, steady boy. He will have his own business some day. And he likes you such a lot."

That little scene with her mother flashed through Ginger's mind as she stood, looking down at Jimmy.

Jimmy started slowly to get up from the floor. "Mary tells me you're going out this evening, so I thought I'd come over and put on your make-up for you." He moved toward her with his greasy hands outstretched.

"Jimmy Daley, don't you dare!" With a little squeal Ginger covered her face. "Mother, don't let him!"

The three of them laughed together as Jimmy gave up. "Say, I understand you got the evening wrap I sent you," he smiled.

"What do you mean, 'you sent me'?" Ginger's eyes were wide in momentary belief.

Then she saw that he was fooling.

"I told him about the cloak," Mary explained a little guiltily.

"Oh, *that* thing." Now was the time to convince her mother that she had never taken the cloak seriously.

"But it's really beautiful," Mary said, surprisingly. "Do you want to see it, Jimmy?"

The telephone rang. As Ginger went to answer it, Mary followed her and went on to Ginger's bedroom.

Miles Harrington's voice answered Ginger's "Hello."

"I'm at the florist's," he said. "What color gown are you wearing tonight?"

Ginger laughed. "It will be a black lace, Miles, in fact, *the* black lace."

"Oh, black lace," he repeated and his tone dropped with disappointment. "I found some lovely things in an odd shade of blue here. I hoped—well, they'd look stunning on red, or—"

"*Red?*"

"Yes. Don't you have something red? You know, Ginger, with that hair and those blue eyes, you should go in for shades of red, or, maybe, bright scarlet."

"*Scarlet?*" Ginger was puzzled. "It's funny that you should say that, Miles, for I have a scarlet opera cloak right here."

"Then why not wear it?" Miles was excited. "I'll send these blue things and you'll be a picture."

Ginger hardly knew how to explain. It would be too long-drawn-out and Miles could not be expected to understand, since no one else did. She suddenly wished she had not mentioned it.

"I can't wear it. You see—well, I don't know where it came from, and Mother—" she began, haltingly.

"It's yours, isn't it?"

"I suppose it is." Oh, why had she told him? "But we don't know who sent it to me, so—"

Miles was decisive. "Look, I'll send out the blue flowers and we'll talk about the cloak when I get there. You'll wear it when you see how these posies look on it. How's seven o'clock? We'll have a quick snack at the Brown Derby and then, after the show, remember, we're going dancing. We can dine as we dance."

When Ginger turned from the telephone, Mary was standing behind her, holding the cloak and dress by the hanger. She asked almost reproachfully, "He wants you to wear it?"

"Yes, but I'm not going to. I don't even know why I told him about it. It's all so silly," Ginger replied.

Mary was unconvinced. "But you hung it like this yourself. You want to wear it, don't you?"

"Of course not, Mother."

Jimmy came through the swinging door. He had washed his hands and pushed back his hair.

"Hey, is this it? Whew, it is a knock-out, isn't it? I'll betchu my socks you wear it tonight."

Seeing the concern in her mother's face, Ginger looked up at Jimmy holding her nose in mock distaste. "If

Mother is willing to hold the stakes, be prepared to lose a pair of socks, my fine-feathered friend."

Mary returned to Ginger's bedroom with her burden of finery. Her heart was immeasurably lightened.

Ginger and Jimmy went to the front porch and sat in the swinging divan, talking of nothing and everything until it was time for Ginger to start dressing. Then Jimmy went home to dinner.

A little later the flowers came and Mary received them at the door. When she took them in to Ginger, she opened the box. Together they exclaimed over the beautiful shade of blue and, while neither spoke of it, both had a womanly desire to see their powdery loveliness nestled against the scarlet collar. Mary took the box of flowers to the kitchen and put them in the refrigerator until it was time for Ginger to go.

A half hour later Ginger sauntered into the living room, dressed and ready. Mary came from the kitchen to join her.

"Thanks, Mommie, for pressing the dress," Ginger said, as Mary made the usual motherly adjustments.

Over the black lace gown Ginger wore the little white satin evening wrap which Mary had made from a pattern in a woman's home magazine.

As Mary looked at Ginger, she thought, in spite of herself, that the scarlet cloak would mean the difference between just another girl in the crowd, and one of the best dressed. But Ginger had apparently closed her mind to any further thought of the cloak and seemed completely happy.

"I'll get the flowers and pin them on."

Mary went to the kitchen and returned with them just as Miles Harrington bounded up the front steps and rang the bell.

Ginger opened the door and greeted him. Then she turned for Mary to pin on her corsage. Miles's expression, when he saw the white wrap, stopped both women in their tracks.

"But you can't—I mean, I thought you were going to wear the scarlet cloak."

Miles was unexplainably disturbed for a moment. Then quickly he changed and began to laugh. Why had she tricked him like that? Why did she let him send the blue flowers? Red flowers should be on the shoulder of a white coat. A splash of red on the white would have exonerated his good taste. But why not wear the scarlet cloak?

Together, Mary and Ginger tried to explain. Miles would listen to none of it. They were being prudish, really. Mary surely knew it was all right. Let him see the cloak. Mary brought it out.

How it all happened she would never be able to remember, but ten minutes later Ginger was walking out the door to Miles's car clad in the scarlet cloak, with the blue flowers pinned on the shoulder, and Mary was standing, smiling, in the doorway, with the white satin wrap draped over her arm. Miles was fairly pushing her, and, when they were in the car, he started off with such speed that Ginger's head was snapped back. She hardly had time to wave to Mary, who was waving at them from the door.

Once around the corner and onto the boulevard, Miles slowed the car. He seemed to settle back and compose himself. Then he looked at her.

"What a difference clothes make. Now you look like an international beauty, little Ginger Rogers!" he said.

Ginger smiled at him. "Do I?"

"I'm going to be proud I was lucky enough to be your escort tonight."

Ginger wondered suddenly if Miles was a snob about clothes.

"You wouldn't have been so proud if I'd worn the other coat?" she asked.

Miles hesitated a moment, then said with a faint smile, "It did sound like that, didn't it?" His eyes were on the road. After a moment he added, "But you know better. Did I ask you what you were going to wear when I invited you?"

"I'm sorry," she said under her breath.

Without looking at her Miles asked, "Will you promise me something, Ginger?"

"What?"

"Will you promise me that you will wear that lovely wrap whenever I want you to?" There seemed to be so much importance to the pause as he waited for her answer.

"Why, I suppose so. Why?"

As she watched the side of his face, his chin lifted slightly. He seemed to have scored some kind of a triumph. What kind she could not decide.

"Because—well, I'm going to ask you to go out with me every day you have off from now on. Will you?" he asked.

How odd, she thought to herself. His question lacked the ring or warmth of romance.

"You mean wear this once a week? It's pretty colorful for that, isn't it? You might get tired of—"

"I won't ask you to wear it every time we go out." He still wouldn't look at her. "Just whenever I want you to. Will you?"

"I'm to promise?"

"Yes."

"Oh, all right. Why not? I love wearing it. But the promise stands only if Mother doesn't change her mind about it in the meantime. I wouldn't want to hurt her."

This would be a way out of her promise, if she wanted a way out, and she considered it rather a stroke of genius.

But Miles caught her thought. "Your mother will let you wear it if *I* want you to."

His downright confidence in his powers of persuasion where her mother was concerned annoyed Ginger. She wanted to defend Mary's weakening under his pressing arguments tonight. But she was speechless before that something in his manner which she could not understand, that careful guarding of his reason for his strange insistence.

At the Brown Derby, Miles turned his car over to the attendant at the door and they entered Hollywood's famous eating place. It was filled to standing room with others who, like themselves, were dressed for the première. As she scanned the room, Ginger recognized many faces she had seen on the screen. When they followed the waiter to the booth which Miles had ordered earlier in the day, she became conscious of eyes glancing at her, then returning to look again.

Complete satisfaction with himself and with the impression which she had made was in Miles's every movement. With an extra flourish he took the cloak from her shoulders and gently placed it on the back of the booth. He looked at her with a nice twinkle in his eyes, and suddenly she felt at home in these new and untried surroundings.

Miles bowed here and there. Evidently he was well-known in this Hollywood set. Eyes turned in their direction and one young woman practically stood up in her booth the better to see the new girl whom Miles was displaying to them.

As the waitress left with their order, a very personable young man appeared beside their table and stopped. Standing as best he could in such a tight-fitting booth, Miles exchanged greetings with him, then introduced Ginger. His name was Jacques Tournier. Their conversation made no sense to Ginger and she found herself growing uncomfortable under the young man's close scrutiny. Again and again, as he talked with Miles, his

Miles Took the Cloak From Her Shoulders

open staring forced her own eyes downward. It was a new experience and she turned to Miles for reassurance. But Miles was talking to his friend in French now, shutting her out completely. She was glad, when, with a little bow, the man left.

"Just a writer friend of mine," Miles explained. "I knew him in Paris. You are quite the hit of the evening, young woman, as I knew you would be. Already the wise ones have placed you as a Broadway actress here to try pictures, or something equally exciting. Anyway, they *know* you are somebody of importance and you *do* look it."

"Well, I certainly don't feel it!"

Ginger didn't. She had never known this brand of confusion before. It made her wish that she could bolt from the place and climb upon her high stool in the telephone room in the quiet of her own familiar world. She saw her fingers toying with the handle of a fork. She pulled her hand away. She knew she would drop it if she picked it up. She felt overwhelmingly gawky and self-conscious.

Then she laughed. That was Ginger's saving grace. She could laugh at herself. The little inward chuckle bubbled up. She took a long breath. It was over, thank goodness! Now they could all stare and gaze and peek and babble to their hearts' content. She was herself again.

A half hour later she marched beside Miles down the roped-off avenue in front of the theatre, where hundreds of fans were gathered to catch a glimpse of their favorite screen stars. With hundreds of eyes following her and hundreds of voices questioning her identity, she never turned a hair. She felt like a veteran actress.

Their seats were much too far forward in the theatre. Ginger wondered at this, since Miles always seemed capable of getting anything he wanted. But, then, he might be near-sighted. At least, they were on the aisle.

While she removed her gloves and prepared once more to drop the scarlet cloak over the back of a seat, she looked directly into the eyes of a man sitting across the aisle, two rows down. He had turned completely around and was staring at her.

The eyes were set in the most evil face she had ever seen. It fascinated her with its satanic wickedness. With slumping shoulders and tilted body, he seemed to be awaiting only a glint of recognition from her before hurling himself across the intervening space between them. An involuntary shudder passed through her. The space between them seemed to lessen as she gazed. Then Miles said something to her and the spell was broken.

The lights dimmed out, but in the glow from the screen she saw the man turn again and again to look back. It broke the continuity of the screen story for her and she could not have told, afterward, whether the picture was good, bad or indifferent. Miles, beside her, seemed restless and constantly stirring. The thread of the story kept getting mixed up with what was going on about her and, try as she might, she could not keep her mind off the man two rows ahead.

When the picture was finished amid thundering applause and the lights had gone up, Miles seemed to grow more nervous. He dropped the program and reached down to pick it up. He nearly put her cloak on wrong side out. He stumbled clumsily against the arm of the seat as he stepped back to let her precede him up the aisle. Ginger wondered what could have gone wrong with Miles. Perhaps he had seen the ugly, little man and resented his staring, blaming it, somehow, on her.

The crowd moved slowly toward the rear of the theatre, visiting together and discussing the picture as they went. Finally Ginger and Miles reached the doorway that opened into the foyer. It was not so crowded there. People were moving more rapidly into the patio and on into the street, where the attendant was calling their cars through a microphone.

Finally, when they were standing in an open space, Ginger saw Miles pull a package of cigarettes from his left-hand coat pocket. As she watched, he dropped them, or rather, let them slip from his hand to the floor.

As quick as a flash the man with the face of Satan appeared from nowhere. He scooped up the package with a motion that was neither stooping nor leaning. With a leering smile, he handed a package of cigarettes to Miles. His movements were birdlike and quick, like the deceiving movements of a sleight-of-hand artist passing things before your eyes.

But Ginger had seen.

Miles accepted the package with a smothered, "Thank you," and, taking Ginger's arm in a too-tight hold, hurried her out into the patio.

Ginger hung back. She wanted to tell Miles what she
had seen, but he seemed not to want to listen. Once outside she stopped him by the simple expedient of standing
still and looking back.

The little man was nowhere to be seen.

"Miles, that man didn't give you *your* package of cigarettes." She was going to make him hear her. "He gave
you one he had in his hand. He kept *your* package."

Rather rudely, she thought, Miles turned her about and
propelled her forward again.

"You're seeing things!" he said.

He took the pack of cigarettes from the pocket into
which he had hastily stuffed them a moment before.
"Here they are."

"But that *isn't* your package." Ginger was not to be
pacified. "I tell you that man has your package. I saw
two packages in his hand. He switched them and kept
yours."

She wanted to stamp her foot at Miles's stupidity.

Miles stopped and faced her. "It seems to me you're
being a little silly. This is my package of cigarettes. Same
brand. Two gone. Two were gone from my package
when I dropped them. Anyway, what would it matter?
Fair exchange is no robbery. Are you going to make
something of it?"

Ginger was astonished. Then her eyes narrowed. "Yes.
You can take me home, please."

With longer strides than usual she started forward, not
caring whether he walked with her or not.

Miles caught up with her.

"Oh, please, Ginger." His voice was apologetic. "I'm so sorry. I was rude. I don't know why, really." He handed his car check to the attendant and turned again to her. "Don't go home. We were to go dancing, remember? I want to dance with you."

As he spoke, she realized the insignificance of the incident and felt ashamed that she had made so much of it. She didn't want to answer him then, for she had a great need to protect her pride. Their car was coming to the curb. It saved her for the time.

Miles put her in and sat in the driver's seat. He pulled away from the curb and headed west. They had turned into Sunset Boulevard before he ventured further comment.

Regretfully he said, "I had so wanted you to have a lovely time, tonight. At least, I had planned that you should."

Ginger didn't answer. She had not had a "lovely time!" If this were one of the "chances any girl would give her eyes for," as Patsy had said, other girls could have them. She had experienced so many emotions tonight, and so many of them unpleasant, that she was tired. Really, she'd rather be sitting at home on the porch divan with Jimmy Daley, just gabbing and giggling.

Then an astonishing thought touched her:

"It's this scarlet cloak! That's what it is! *I'll never wear it again!*"

CHAPTER FIVE

FACED WITH TRAGEDY

Ginger Rogers walked through the main entrance into the dimly lighted foyer of the Mocambo. Rhythmic strains of rhumba music floated out to her as she stood waiting for Miles to check his coat with the pretty little girl in the French maid's costume. What she could see of the main dining room resembled a colorful flower bed of dazzling evening gowns. She recognized faces she had seen before that evening at the Brown Derby and at the theater.

Ginger viewed the scene with passive indifference. While Miles had convinced her of the folly of spoiling their well-planned evening, he had not succeeded in dispelling the feeling that she was going places and doing things she shouldn't. She half wished herself away from the Mocambo and at home where she could think clearly.

At such a moment and in such a place, almost any other girl in the world would have been thrilled and excited. But Ginger wasn't thrilled. She wasn't excited. She wasn't even impressed or interested. She had had enough fun for one night. This was going to be the surfeiting portion of whipped cream on a delicious dessert.

When Miles stepped to her side, she suddenly thought of her cloak.

"Do you want to check this?" she asked, unfastening it at the throat.

Quickly Miles stopped her.

"No, I want you to wear it in there. I want you to make an entrance," he told her as he smiled at her proudly.

"Yes, Mr. Harrington," the head waiter was saying to them from the level of the main floor, two steps below. "Right this way."

Ginger followed the head waiter down the steps and through the broad archway that opened into the lavish expanse of the famous Hollywood night club. On the far side of the room a bank of wide windows framed a view of the neon-lighted city at its feet. In the middle of the room, in front of a draped bandstand, a dance floor the size of a pocket handkerchief was crowded with couples.

The head waiter led Ginger and Miles to a table at the edge of the dance floor's far corner. When Ginger was seated she could see every nook and cranny of the room and everyone in it. The table had most certainly been chosen with an eye to seeing and being seen. Even in her own inexperience in such matters, Ginger knew this was the best and most conspicuous table in the room. In her present mood, however, she would have preferred one of the booths against the wall or one of the twosomes in a corner by a window.

Miles ordered the dinner for them both. The music stopped. The dancers left the floor. Ginger settled herself in her chair and surveyed the room.

Suddenly her eyes were drawn toward one of the

booths. Someone was smiling at her, silently saying, "Hello!" Her heart lifted and jumped a beat.

It was Gregg Phillips.

Boldly he blew a kiss to her. She nearly sent one back in her unexpected joy at seeing him, but caught herself just in time. The chill of her former mood disappeared. Nothing had changed in the room, but suddenly everything seemed brighter, as though someone had turned on more light. She was warm inside. She was glad she had come.

Miles was watching her.

"Do you know *him?*" he asked in a displeased voice.

"Gregg Phillips? Yes, of course." The happy glow still lighted her eyes.

"So do I." Miles hesitated a moment and his eyes grew hard and sharp. "I don't like him. And he's not the kind of a man you should know."

"Why?" Ginger asked, completely surprised.

"Because he's a playboy," Miles snapped without further hesitation. "He imagines himself a whiz with the women. He has a very bad reputation."

Ginger dropped her eyes in embarrassed annoyance. She wanted to say something in defense of Gregg, something sharp and biting. But how could she know that Miles was wrong? There were men like that in the world, probably, though she had never met one. Gregg could easily be a spoiled egotist with his social position and his looks. But she didn't believe it. You couldn't associate cheapness with Gregg Phillips' frank, ingenuous manner and boyish smile.

Still Ginger realized that she had talked with Gregg, face to face, only a few times and that, at those times, they had said nothing of importance. *"No!"* she told herself. She wouldn't doubt Gregg. Something had passed between them when they met. It was a wordless understanding which joined them in a bond of faith and confidence. She felt as if she had always known him, had always trusted him and would continue to trust him forever.

Ginger habitually relied upon her instincts in judging people. Of course, she had never been associated with this social class before. But why should they be different? They were just people, like the boys and girls at school, the men and women in the neighborhood, and the girls with whom she worked. She had always chosen her friends for their personal merits. So, until she had some proof against the good character of Gregg Phillips, she would follow the dictates of her intuition and continue to like and admire him.

Miles was speaking.

"The gray-haired man with Gregg is J. Bronson Bagnall, the head of my department at Spurlock Aircraft. He lives at your hotel," he said.

"Yes, I know," Ginger answered indifferently.

"You mean, you know him, too?"

This was too much! Her impatience with Miles's ungraciousness was not concealed in her crisp reply.

"I only meant I know that Mr. Bagnall lives at the

Gregg Phillips and Mr. Bagnall Sat Near By

Seaview Arms. I handle phone calls for him."

What an unpleasant person Miles was turning out to be!

"Does it matter?" she added after a brief pause.

Although Miles smiled, ready to relieve the tension with a humorous remark, he was not given the opportunity. At that moment the head waiter leaned over his shoulder and placed a folded bit of paper close to his hand, muttering something which Ginger did not hear.

It was plain at once that Miles was surprised. He said: "Pardon me."

Then his eyes searched the room. The expression on his face showed that he did not find whom or what he sought.

"Pardon me," he said again.

Still protecting the paper in a cupped hand, he furtively looked around him, as if to make sure that no one was standing near. Then he unfolded the paper and read what must have been a very short note indeed; it took him such a few swift seconds to scan it.

Ginger watched, fascinated. She was not curious about the note. She was interested in the lightning changes of expression on the face of the strange young man who was her escort for the evening. Miles was giving her a new impression of himself every minute.

She had had little experience in the world beyond her own circle, so she had no yardstick by which to measure a person as changeable as Miles. But her instincts were alive. She had dismissed any thoughts of adding Miles to her list of friends. She watched him with merely an impersonal interest.

As Miles quickly read the note, his face clouded with mixed emotions. He ran an uncertain hand through his sleek black hair. Then he crumpled the note and jammed it into his jacket pocket.

"This is—this is—awkward," he explained jerkily, ill at ease. "It's a—a friend—probably a touch. Would you mind very much—that is, I've got to go out and see him for a moment. . . . Do you mind sitting alone for a little while?"

Ginger had a fleeting feeling that Miles was afraid of something.

She was quick to give the assurance that she felt Miles needed at the moment.

"Of course not," she said.

Without another word Miles stood up and left.

As interested as she had been, Ginger found no ready explanation for Miles's strange actions, so she stopped thinking about them, now that he was gone. To her dismay, she found that she *did* mind sitting alone. At the table, which was so conspicuously placed, she was completely surrounded by staring eyes.

A waiter placed a tall glass of lemonade before her. He put another glass at Miles's place.

"Thank you," she said with a forced smile.

The white-coated man neither answered nor looked at her, but disappeared as quickly as he had come, leaving Ginger embarrassingly alone.

She was thirsty. Surely it would be all right if she just sipped her lemonade. But no, she must be polite and wait for Miles to return. Well, he probably would be back in a minute or two.

But five tedious, long-drawn-out, self-conscious minutes passed and still Miles had not come back. Finally the orchestra, coming onto the stage after a brief rest period, swung into a tuneful popular air. People swarmed like flies, two by two, from every direction onto the dance floor. Ginger was grateful. With the dance floor crowded she would not be so set apart, and she could amuse herself by looking at the pretty dresses.

Her relief was short-lived, however, for the dancers were taking this opportunity to get a closer view of her as they glided by her table. *Where was Miles?* Couldn't a girl just get up and go home at a time like this?

Then, suddenly, Gregg Phillips was standing beside her.

"You know, Seven, you were never meant to be alone," he smiled.

Ginger's spirits took wing. The room, the dancers, her troubled thoughts vanished. All at once she was where she ought to be, with Gregg. She offered no resistance as he took her gently by one wrist and pulled her to her feet. He put an arm about her waist and led her out on the dance floor.

"This is swell," Gregg said as they circled the floor.

Their feet moved together, as if wound on the same spring. They swayed with one motion, as if they had danced their whole lives together.

Then Gregg saw Ginger turn her head in the direction of her table. He looked, too. It was still deserted.

"Don't worry, honey," he said, smiling mischievously. "When he comes back, I'll ask him for this dance. He'll have to say 'yes,' won't he?"

"Supposing he says 'no'?" she teased.

"He'll have to learn, sooner or later, that he can't leave you alone in a room with me." Gregg drew her closer to him. "Everybody will have to learn that, sooner or later."

It was wonderful. Ginger wanted to snuggle into his arms and forget everything and everybody. She did. She fitted there, she belonged there—and she knew that he felt the same way. To herself she sang the words of the romantic song the orchestra was playing. It might have been chosen for their special benefit. Gregg seemed to be singing inside, too, for he hummed a line of the words aloud.

After a graceful turn Gregg threw back his head and laughed with sheer enjoyment.

"You're terrific!" he whispered.

The music stopped. The dancers started back to their tables. Still Ginger's table, with its two untouched drinks and the scarlet cloak thrown carelessly over the back of one of the chairs, remained unoccupied.

"Come over to my table," Gregg suggested, leading Ginger that way. "Let me introduce you to Mr. Bagnall. He's such a nice person. I'm sure you'll like him. He already likes you."

"I want to meet him," Ginger said.

As they approached the booth where Mr. Bagnall sat, Ginger saw a man who, when he stood up, must be several degrees above middle height. He was broad of shoulder and sun-tanned to a leathery brown. He had a shock of white curly hair and brown eyes, well set apart. As he smiled, Ginger saw two rows of strong, white teeth.

Mr. Bagnall's smile broadened in anticipation as they came up to him. He stood as Gregg introduced him to Ginger.

Ginger slid into the booth beside Mr. Bagnall and Gregg sat on her other side. Gregg motioned for a waiter.

"Please bring that dolled-up lemonade from that table," he said. Then he turned to the others. "We only guaranteed to entertain her, J. B. There's nothing in our contract that says we're to feed her, too."

They all laughed.

"Where did Miles go?" Mr. Bagnall asked. "It isn't like him to leave you alone for so long."

Ginger told them about the note, and Mr. Bagnall's brow clouded.

"Well, he'll come back. We can be sure of that, when we look at the young lady we have so conveniently kidnaped," Mr. Bagnall smiled. "And, may I add that, besides being very lovely, this young lady is a most competent business woman."

His words were not flattery; they were sincere.

"Thank you, Mr. Bagnall," Ginger bobbed her shining head. "It has been a pleasure to be of service to you."

"Can I get into this mutual admiration society, or are all the seats taken?" Gregg interrupted. "I want to go on record, Mr. Bagnall. I have designs on this lovely young lady, and I want no interference from the gray-haired section. Is that clear?"

"Clear enough." Mr. Bagnall raised his glass. "Success to you! But don't be surprised if you're the one who has to walk home."

The next half hour was gay with their banter and merry laughter. Ginger's self-consciousness disappeared and she was as comfortable as if she were at home in her own living room. Yet all three, each in a personal and special way, kept watch on the table across the room.

As the minutes passed, and still Miles did not return, Mr. Bagnall grew serious. He laughed less frequently and sometimes he seemed not to hear the quips and jokes of the other two.

At last he said, "I think, if you two young people will pardon an old man who has to get up early in the morning, I'll just run along home. With me gone you can do some more stepping to that wonderful music."

Ginger glanced at her wrist watch and said, "It's getting late. I should be going home, too. You go out my way, Mr. Bagnall. I live between here and the Seaview Arms. You could drop me off, couldn't you?"

There was a moment's hesitation before Mr. Bagnall said, in some embarrassment, "Why, of course—I—"

He looked at Gregg helplessly.

Gregg spoke up quickly.

"Oh, no you don't! When there's taking home to be done, *I'm* the boy. Besides, Mr. Bagnall came in my chariot and he's goin' home with the guy what brung 'im."

Mr. Bagnall laughed and there was relief in his laughter.

Gregg added, "There's a white moon shining, too, and that means Mr. Bagnall goes home first. Since you're in such a hurry, you'll like that, eh, Mr. B.?"

They were leaving the booth and Mr. Bagnall did not answer.

"I suppose this is the only thing I can do under the circumstances—I mean, go home. Surely Miles wouldn't expect me to go on waiting here. . . ." Ginger said uncertainly.

"Don't you worry your little head about a thing, honey. You're absolutely right," Gregg said with firm assurance.

Ginger saw the quick look which passed between the two men. Mr. Bagnall seemed to be telling Gregg something with his eyes. Gregg evidently understood the unspoken message, whatever it was.

Now Mr. Bagnall seemed to be in a hurry. He took one of Ginger's hands and guided her through the maze of tables, zigzagging until they reached the dance floor. Gregg had taken her other hand, and they walked three abreast until they reached the deserted table and the scarlet cloak.

Mr. Bagnall held the cloak and Ginger quickly slipped

A Quick Look Passed Between the Men

into it. Then they made their way to the foyer. Gregg stopped to press a bill into the head waiter's hand and Ginger overheard enough to understand that he was paying Miles's check.

"Bless him," she said to herself and a warm thrill passed through her whole being as she watched him.

With his long easy stride he mounted the stairs and returned to her side. For a breathless moment he looked down into her eyes. He took her hand and squeezed it gently. Then he laughed again, that low triumphant laugh of sheer happiness which Ginger was learning to love. It said so much, that laugh. It said, *"I love you."* It said, *"Every time you look at me like that I know I've won a little more ground with you."* And it said, *"Every little bit added to what you've already got makes just a little bit more."*

"Bless him," Ginger said again, silently.

Ginger and Gregg followed Mr. Bagnall to the sidewalk. After Gregg handed the doorman the check for his car, Mr. Bagnall stepped up to the doorman and spoke to him in a low tone. Ginger could not hear what Mr. Bagnall said, but the doorman answered in a loud voice.

"Yes, sir. About an hour ago Mr. Harrington came out and another fella met him here. Mr. Harrington called for his car and, as he and the other man got in, Mr. Harrington said to me, 'Hey, Dick, tell the little lady in the scarlet cloak. . . .'" The doorman paused and turned to Ginger. "I guess he meant you, miss. . . . ."

Ginger nodded.

Mr. Bagnall was impatient.

"But what did he tell you to say to the little lady in the scarlet cloak?" he demanded waspishly.

"Nothin'. You see, the other fella, who was with him, motioned him to drive on. So they drove on. He didn't finish what he'd intended to say, I guess."

Mr. Bagnall and Gregg exchanged quick glances, heavy with meaning.

Gregg asked, "Which way did they go from here? Did you notice?"

"Yes, sir. Mr. Harrington drove up to the next corner and turned around. Then they drove by here again on the other side of the street, headed out Sunset Boulevard."

At that moment Gregg's car came to the curb. Hurriedly Mr. Bagnall tucked Ginger into the seat while Gregg went round to the steering-wheel side. Then Mr. Bagnall got in beside Ginger. Not a word was spoken. Gregg sped away from the curb and turned around in the middle of the block in bland defiance of all traffic regulations. Heading out Sunset Boulevard, gathering speed as they went, they were going in the direction of Ginger's home, as well as toward the Seaview Arms. But somehow, Ginger felt that there was another destination in the minds of the two silent men beside her.

It was Gregg who first spoke:

"All right, boss. Let's have it."

"The nearest telephone," Mr. Bagnall said, tersely; then he added, "Everything is closed. I suppose the Seaview Arms is really the best place, and the safest."

"How about the Beverly Hills police station?" Gregg asked, not taking his eyes off the road.

"No—not yet," Mr. Bagnall answered. "The hotel. There may be messages for me. . . ."

"I get it," Gregg answered and pressed his foot harder on the accelerator.

Their conversation had not included her, but Ginger could not resist saying, "If there are messages I could get them for you, Mr. Bagnall. Patsy's on the board."

She had not intended to intrude on their problem. Although she knew that their concern had to do with Miles, she would not ask questions. Mr. Bagnall's business was important, secret and governmental. She wanted to know only what he wanted her to know. But she was involved in this matter and she was anxious to help if she could.

Mr. Bagnall did not seem surprised. He answered as if he were talking to Gregg.

"No, I think we'd better arouse as little suspicion as possible. All this must be kept secret, understand, until we know what's what. Then it must be doubly secret."

Again Ginger had to speak.

"When we get there, I could run up to the board and handle your calls for you. Then no one would ever know about anything."

"That's not a bad idea, J. B.," Gregg said. "If it's a false alarm, it would die right there."

"It's no false alarm, Gregg," Mr. Bagnall said.

There was the sadness and disappointment in his voice of a man betrayed. After a moment he added:

"Yes, it might be well for Ginger to handle all the calls."

Ginger said, "You see, Mr. Bagnall, you can give me the names before I go up, then no one will know whom I'm dialing, not even Patsy. The names needn't even be spoken over the wires. You can just say 'call number one' or 'call number two.'"

They were turning into Palisades Boulevard, the wide street which crowns the brow of the Palisades along the seashore. At its end it meets the winding motor roads, paths, and walks of the Seaview Arms.

The white moon cast into dark shadows the tall palms which lined the Boulevard. The hotel was just ahead.

Suddenly the headlights of Gregg's car picked up another car, parked at an awkward angle on the wrong side of the street. Gregg was turning out to miss it when Ginger called excitedly:

"That's Miles's car!"

Gregg stepped on the brakes so suddenly that the other two were thrown against the windshield. Mr. Bagnall grabbed Ginger to keep her from being unseated as the tires came to a screaming stop.

Quickly Gregg pulled his own car to the front of the other and turned on his spotlight. The three clambered swiftly out of the car.

The curb-side door of Miles's automobile stood open—and the car itself was empty.

"You're sure this is Miles's car, Ginger?" Gregg asked, hurriedly examining it.

"Yes, I'm positive," she asserted; after all, she ought to know it.

"This is the car he checked at the Mocambo?" Mr. Bagnall asked.

"Yes. This is it."

"Look!"

The exclamation came from Gregg. He had opened the glove compartment, found a flashlight and turned the beam of light onto the cushions, dashboard, and steering wheel.

"Blood!" Mr. Bagnall exclaimed.

The steering wheel was smeared with still-wet red. Great red drops gleamed on the floor in the piercing light.

"That means—"

Mr. Bagnall didn't finish. He swung away from the car and began a quick survey of the ground and curb.

"Here, Gregg, bring the flashlight."

As Gregg came round from the other side, his swinging flash caught wheel marks on the street. He stopped to trace them with the beam.

"That car was out of control, J. B.!" he cried. "It was headed the same way we are, went over to the curb opposite, then swung, almost on two wheels, to where it now stands."

"Bring the light," was all Mr. Bagnall said.

He took it and flashed it on the curb and ground. The light followed a trail of blood that led to the right toward the sidewalk. There the trail seemed to end. A little farther on, he picked it up again.

He turned to Gregg. "Have you some gloves with you?"

"There's a pair in my car," Gregg answered.

"Put them on. Get into Miles's car. Be very careful, Gregg. Turn it around and park it by the curb so it won't attract attention. Park your own car behind it and turn out all the lights. Quick! We've been lucky so far. If a cruising police car should come along. . . ."

"I get it!" Gregg bounded off.

Ginger followed Mr. Bagnall. The trail of blood left the sidewalk and turned into a hedge that completely covered a woven-wire fence lining the south end of the Seaview Arms' gardens. The trail ran along the fence, away from it and back again. Mr. Bagnall and Ginger ducked under low-hanging branches and pressed on beside the hedge. The parted leaves showed that someone had gone through before them. Ginger dared not think what they might find.

Following the gleam from the flashlight, Gregg caught up with them.

"It's done, J. B. I parked both cars in front of that big house back there. There are lights still on in the house, so the cars look okay there."

Suddenly Mr. Bagnall switched off the light. He stood still and held up one hand.

Ginger and Gregg froze in their tracks.

The gleam of a flashlight came through the leaves and branches from the other side of the hedge.

Then a deep voice asked, "Who's there?"

After what seemed an eternity of doubt and uncertainty, Gregg answered, "It's me. Is that you, Charlie?"

Gregg was holding Ginger's arm in a vise-like grip and she knew he meant that she should keep still. Mr. Bagnall seemed poised in mid-air. They held their breath waiting for the answer.

It came.

"No, this is John Hines. Who are you?"

John Hines was the night watchman for the Seaview Arms.

With a sigh of relief Gregg answered, "Oh, John, it's I, Gregg Phillips."

"Well, what in tarnation are you doing back there?"

Gregg was thinking fast. Ginger heard him swallow hard before he answered.

"I lost my wrist watch this afternoon. I wanted to find it before someone else ran across it," he said.

"I heard you talking. Is someone with you?" John Hines asked, throwing the beam of his flash through the hedgerow.

The closely-knit branches of the hedge prevented his seeing through the thick leaves. The three on the other side sighed with silent thankfulness.

"Yes, Mr. Bagnall is with me," Gregg replied. "He's helping me look."

Mr. Bagnall switched on his light and circled it about the ground to keep up the pretense of searching.

The light shot ahead. There, lying in a pool of blood almost at their very feet, was Miles Harrington!

CHAPTER SIX

SOMETHING MYSTERIOUS

A violent chill ran through Ginger's body. Gregg heard her shaking gasp and pulled her toward him, holding her face against his breast to smother a possible scream.

Mr. Bagnall swerved the flashlight beam away from the prostrate body and turned in the opposite direction.

"Yes, I'm here too, John," he said quietly and calmly. Gregg pulled himself together.

"John, will you look on that side of the hedge? It's a gold watch with a gold wristband. Your flashlight will pick it out easily if it's there."

How could they be so calm, Ginger was thinking, with Miles lying dead at their feet?

Mr. Bagnall knelt, worming his body into a position between the figure on the ground and the prying eyes beyond the hedge. He turned the light into Miles's face. A dark smear covered Miles's forehead, and his hair was matted with drying blood that had run in rivulets down his face.

"Sure, I'll look," John Hines said. "But how do you figure it got over there if you lost it over here?"

Ginger knew that Gregg was performing another feat of mental gymnastics. "I was throwing a ball, John," he

95

said after a moment's hesitation. "The watch went with it. I couldn't tell where it fell. The sun was in my eyes. I thought maybe it flew over the hedge. It could have, you know."

"Yeah, I guess it could," John answered.

The flashlight on the other side of the hedge played on the grass as John Hines searched for the missing watch.

Silently Mr. Bagnall handed his flashlight to Gregg. He made a circling motion with his hand. Gregg followed the silent instructions, bringing the beam to rest on Mr. Bagnall and Miles as often and as long as he dared with each circling motion.

Mr. Bagnall put a hand inside Miles's coat.

"He's alive!" he whispered.

"Dear Lord, thank you." Ginger was not conscious that she had whispered her prayer aloud.

Gregg heard and drew her closer to him.

Mr. Bagnall put an arm under Miles's shoulders. In a flash of the light Ginger and Gregg saw Miles's eyelids flutter. His lips moved.

In a low and childlike murmur that brought tears to Ginger's eyes, he was saying over and over:

"*Grand-mère embrasse moi. Grand-mère embrasse moi.*"

Ginger turned to Gregg, whispering, "What is he saying? It's French, isn't it?"

"Yes," answered Gregg, "He's delirious. He's saying, '*Oh, grandmother, take me in your arms,*' or something like that. Sounds like a little boy, doesn't he?"

Mr. Bagnall Put an Arm Under Miles's Shoulders

"Yes."

Ginger's heart ached with pity. She had come to dislike Miles heartily that evening. But now, seeing him helpless and injured and hearing him calling like a child for a grandmother who could not know he needed her so much, brought the tears to her eyes. All her antipathy was washed away. She wanted to do something, anything, to help him.

She knelt down beside Mr. Bagnall, whispering, "Can't I do something?"

Mr. Bagnall shook his head.

Gregg leaned across her and whispered to Mr. Bagnall, "What can we do now, boss?"

"We've got to get him out of here and take him to a doctor," Mr. Bagnall replied in a low voice. "There's a nasty cut across his head that needs sewing up."

"Okay." Gregg murmured.

Mr. Bagnall whispered again:

"Be careful, Gregg. Remember, no one must know about this!"

Gregg nodded in understanding and stood up. A shaft of moonlight fell across his face. He seemed to take a stance, like an actor in a play, ready to speak his lines.

"Well, I guess it's not here, Mr. Bagnall," he said in a loud voice. "What say we give it up?"

The light in his hand still played in circles on the ground about him.

"Just as you say." Mr. Bagnall's voice matched Gregg's in volume. "But it's a shame we can't find it."

From the pitiful figure on the ground came again that little wail, *"Grand-mère embrasse moi."*

Ginger took one of Miles's hands in both her own.

"There, there," she crooned softly, as if speaking to soothe a restless child.

"Did you find it?" John Hines asked from the other side of the hedge.

"No, John. We're going to give up. I'll come back and look in the morning," Gregg answered. "Thanks for helping."

"You're welcome," John said. "I'll look some more later, but I've got to make my rounds again now."

The two men breathed deeply with relief. The danger of discovery by John was almost past.

"Goodnight, John, and thanks again." Gregg said.

"Goodnight, Mr. Phillips," John replied. "Goodnight, Mr. Bagnall."

"Goodnight, John," Mr. Bagnall said.

Gregg began to lash the branches about him to create the sound effect of their departure.

"This way, Mr. Bagnall," he said loudly, then crouched quickly and peered through the lower branches of the hedge. John's flashlight was receding across the lawn.

"Come on," Gregg said, when John's light had disappeared.

Mr. Bagnall took command.

"Ginger, you take the light. Keep it shut off until we have to have it. We mustn't attract attention. You'd better walk ahead. We'll make it by easy stages. Keep your ears open. If we hear anything, we'll stop. If anyone calls to us, we won't answer —This is a ticklish business. The courts call it 'obstructing justice' and we must not get caught."

He paused for a moment then turned to Gregg.

"Are the keys in your car?" he asked.

"No, J. B. I have them here, in my pocket."

Gregg pulled out the keys.

"Give them to Ginger," Mr. Bagnall instructed.

Without hesitation Gregg obeyed.

"When we get to the sidewalk at the end of this hedge, we will stop and listen," Mr. Bagnall continued. "If there is no one in sight, you walk out to the sidewalk, Ginger. Look carefully in every direction. If you see nothing, begin to whistle a soft tune. Then walk straight to Gregg's car and get it. Can you drive?"

"Yes, I can drive."

"Then drive *straight home!*"

Ginger wanted to protest, but there was absolute finality in Mr. Bagnall's voice. What he said was actually a command.

He continued, "Gregg, you go out next, look around, then get Miles's car and bring it to the curb down here. Stop it, turn out the lights and sit quietly for a few minutes, listening. If all is well, then come and help me. From there on it will be comparatively easy. Is everything clear?"

"Yes, sir," Ginger answered.

"Yes, J. B.," Gregg said.

Gregg lifted Miles's shoulders and Mr. Bagnall grasped his legs. Ginger took her position in front and, when the two men had the limp and unresisting body firmly clasped in their arms, she parted the branches to make way for them.

Ginger was alert in every fiber of her being. Her ears strained to hear any sound, except the crackling of the branches and the rustle of the leaves, as they made their winding way through the underbrush.

Her brain seethed with questions. Who was Miles's assailant? Why had he been attacked so brutally? What did Mr. Bagnall mean when he said that they were "obstructing justice" by rescuing Miles from such a hideous fate? Had somebody tried to murder Miles? Never in her life had Ginger done an unlawful thing, and, if this were wrong, what made it so?

She knew that Mr. Bagnall and Gregg were not the kind of men to be mixed up in anything underhanded. At least, Gregg Phillips wasn't. Her heart told her that. As for Mr. Bagnall, he seemed so stable, high-minded, and patriotic. But Mr. Bagnall knew something about tonight's happenings, something which no one else knew. She felt, instinctively, that he was doing the right thing, whatever his secret knowledge might be.

Ginger's shoulders went back with a pride of being part of it all. "I'm glad I'm here," she said to herself. Then she stopped stone-still.

The men behind her stopped. Not a leaf or branch stirred. In the silence they heard the unmistakable sounds of an idling car motor.

"It's a police car," Gregg whispered.

Through the branches they saw the headlights shining on the street. The car was cruising away from the hotel entrance toward the two cars, parked at the curb a hundred feet ahead.

The three in the bushes held their breath. They could not see clearly through the dank undergrowth. They could only listen. The car went by slowly.

Then their hearts stood still! The sounds of the motor were not diminishing! The car must have stopped beside the other cars, parked in front of the big lighted house.

Ginger wondered whether the occupants of the moving car were the regular patrolmen of this district. If they were, they would probably know the habits of its residents and would be suspicious of the two strange cars parked in front of the big house so late at night.

She had to know for sure, so she started forward. In bending down to avoid a branch, she stepped upon the flowing hem of the scarlet cloak and fell, crashing through the bushes. Sharp twigs scraped her arms and hands and neck. But she didn't notice because, from her prone position on the ground, she could plainly see the two parked cars and the third car, which was slowly passing, its spotlight searching lawns and trees and doors.

The cruising car went slowly on its way and Ginger lay watching until its headlights turned a corner and disappeared. Then she scrambled to her feet.

"Are you hurt?" Gregg whispered anxiously.

"No," she answered. "The car's gone. I watched it."

"This is our chance," Mr. Bagnall murmured thankfully. "Let's go."

Following Mr. Bagnall's instructions, they stood stock still and listened when they reached the end of the hedge. No sound came to them so, with a backward wave of her hand, Ginger held the flashlight out to Mr. Bagnall. He took it. Then Ginger stepped away from the hedge and onto the strip of lawn that edged the walk.

Her heart beat violently. She was alone. She had ceased to be a part of the drama hidden in the hedge. Now she must play a solitary role.

She listened, then stealthily ventured to the sidewalk. She stood there, looking about, her eyes alert for any moving thing. Like a giant searchlight, the moon lit up everything as bright as day—except the deep black shadows of the trees. Ginger's eyes searched these shadows. Satisfied that no one was near, she stepped out on the sidewalk. Her heels clicked loudly on the pavement, like little rifle shots in the still night. She began to tiptoe. Then she remembered that she must whistle. She puckered her lips.

But no sound came forth. She stopped and stood still, frozen into terrified silence.

On the edge of the lawn that sloped from the big house toward the hedge, a man stood silently watching her. His figure was sharply etched in the moonlight. He stood very still, his hands sunk deeply in the pockets of his dressing robe. His feet were encased in carpet slippers.

Ginger's first impulse was to flee. She whirled and the

heavy cloak billowed around her, making a scarlet cloud in the moonlight.

Suddenly and unexpectedly, she laughed! Hysteria and fear were in that laughter and she could not stop.

The man stood motionless, watching her. In the bright light of the moon she could see the disgust in his face. She suddenly realized that he probably thought she was tipsy.

She laughed more loudly, not knowing what else to do. She whirled again and watched the scarlet waves of the cloak, billowing around her.

Suddenly Gregg stepped from the hedge and started up the sidewalk toward her. She came to a standstill, afraid that she might do the wrong thing. She knew, with a blind trust, that Gregg would get her out of this predicament.

In a quavering voice she called, "Come on, Gregg." She was trembling with excitement and suspense.

If Gregg saw the motionless figure standing on the lawn, he gave no sign. Without speaking, he swept Ginger up into his arms and strode toward the cars. He deposited her in his own car, hurried around to the driver's seat and climbed in.

"Give me the keys." His voice was unnatural and strained.

Ginger fumbled with her cloak until she remembered that she had the keys in her hand. Quickly Gregg put one in the lock, but before he could pull away from the curb, the man stood beside the car.

"Whose car is that?"

His voice was gruff and angry and he was pointing toward Miles's car with one hand. His other hand was buried in the robe pocket.

Ginger knew that he was probably clutching a revolver in his hidden hand.

Gregg's answer was as short and gruff as the man's question had been.

"How should I know?"

Gregg threw the car into reverse, backed, then drove forward with a swift lunge.

"Whew!" he exclaimed, when they had reached the driveway entrance of the Seaview Arms at the end of the street. "That was a close call!"

He stopped the car and turned out the lights.

"Oh, Gregg, I'm so sorry," Ginger said weakly.

"Why, darling, it wasn't your fault. You were wonderful! How could you know that guy would be there?" He put his arms around her and pulled her to him. "Why, Ginger, you're shaking like a leaf."

Ginger was afraid she was going to cry. She didn't want to do that. There was so much yet to be done. With all her powers of control she held herself in check.

"What are we going to do, Gregg? We can't just stand here. We've got to get poor Miles to a doctor," she said finally.

"We will, honey." Gregg patted her arm reassuringly. "But we've got to give that big galoot time enough to stop wondering about the car and go in the house where he belongs. He mustn't see or suspect anything. He might call the police."

He looked down at her.

"Scared?"

"I don't think so. Maybe I was, but I'm not now."

"Just hold on a little longer, honey. We'll make another try." Gregg gritted his teeth. "This time it's *got* to work."

Slowly he meshed the gears. At four miles an hour, with lights out, he guided the car back down Palisades Boulevard, hugging the curb on the wrong side of the street. Quietly he pulled up beside the hedge and stopped. Then, like a streak of lightning, he leaped out of the car and into the underbrush.

With straining eyes, Ginger looked up and down the empty street. At her whispered assurance that all was clear, the two men stepped from the hedge with their unconscious burden, circled the car and put Miles in beside her. Ginger slipped over under the wheel.

"That's right," said Mr. Bagnall. "You drive this one, Ginger. Gregg, get that other car and follow us."

He got in on the other side of Miles and whispered to Ginger, "Give me your cloak."

While she slipped out of the scarlet cloak and watched Mr. Bagnall cover the inert body beside her, Ginger was wondering what dangers Gregg might face in following Mr. Bagnall's orders to "get that other car." What if the angry man still stood guard over it?

Sensing her anxiety, Gregg came to her side. He put

The Men Carried the Unconscious Man to the Car

a hand lightly on her arm, whispering:

"Look, honey, keep the lights out. I'm going to step up on the rear bumper and ride until we reach the car, so swing over to it as close as you can. Go slowly, but don't stop for anything. I'll jump off when we're even with the front end. Don't worry."

He gave her arm a little squeeze before he disappeared toward the rear.

Ginger drove slowly toward the other car. She knew when Gregg left the bumper, though she dared not look back.

"Now go over to the right side of the street and turn on your lights and let's get out of here," Mr. Bagnall directed.

Ginger obeyed, scarcely breathing, as she listened for some sound from Gregg.

Then she heard the purr of a motor. Twin lights reflected themselves in the rear-view mirror. Her heart bounded with joy.

"Here he comes! He made it!" Mr. Bagnall said.

They headed back toward Beverly Hills. Mr. Bagnall directed the route.

"I'm sorry I can't drop you at home, Ginger," he apologized. "But I can't drive. We couldn't have managed this without you tonight."

"I'm glad I was along," she said, watching the road.

There was more meaning to her words than Mr. Bagnall could guess, she told herself, as she saw in the mirror the reflected lights of the car Gregg was driving.

Before this night Gregg had been only an amusing acquaintance. But now everything was changed. She really knew him now, knew that he was brave and strong and—

"Strange!"

She said the word aloud, not realizing that she had spoken.

"Yes, it is strange," Mr. Bagnall replied. "But you'll learn, as you grow older, Ginger, that life is much stranger than fiction. Gregg is always in the midst of experiences. We turn here."

She turned.

At this point things began happening fast.

"Now around this corner," Mr. Bagnall directed. "The second house on the right-hand side. Drive into the yard and on through to the back."

She obeyed.

"Now swing out, so Gregg can come in around you."

She followed the directions. Gregg was right behind. He passed her and drove Miles's car into the garage. He leaped out and closed the garage door.

Mr. Bagnall was ringing the back doorbell. Ginger had no idea where she was. In the confusion of winding and turning at Mr. Bagnall's hasty directions, she had lost all sense of direction and she had scarcely noticed the house into whose backyard they had so unceremoniously driven. She had no idea of why they were there. But, as yet, she was not fully aware of the peculiarity of the situation.

She had had little time to think. When Mr. Bagnall had jumped from the car, releasing his hold upon the unconscious man, Miles's shoulders had slid along the back of the leather seat and his head had sunk against her side. Tenderly she had gathered him in her arms to support his sagging head. For the first time, she saw the deep cut that started at the top of his brow and ended far back behind one ear. Though she had only the moon for light, she could see that the blow had evidently been dealt with murderous intent.

Softly she pressed one cool hand to his forehead. He stirred and mumbled something unintelligible, something in French.

Then Ginger heard the opening of the back door of the house. But there was no light. She heard Mr. Bagnall giving a low-voiced and very short explanation to a blank, black doorway.

Then Gregg and Mr. Bagnall lifted Miles from the car and disappeared into the yawning blackness beyond the door. She was left alone, with only the stained and rumpled scarlet cloak as company. Not a light shown from the house. Not a sound came from anywhere. The whole neighborhood was as still as a graveyard.

CHAPTER SEVEN

WHAT WAS NOT TOLD

A chill shook Ginger from head to toe. The December night was heavy with dew, damp and cold. She wrapped the scarlet cloak about her body. Then she thought of her mother. She turned on the dashboard light to see the clock. It was two-thirty. Would Mary be awake and be worried? Then she remembered Miles's warning that she would be home late. Poor Miles! He had had such different plans for their evening.

She thought of the ugly man in the theater and the way he had looked at her. She had a distinct feeling that he had followed them up the aisle. He *had* picked up Miles's cigarettes. She was sure of that because she had seen it with her own eyes. And that little man had looked at her so knowingly, as though she were a recognized confederate in some dark deed he was perpetrating. The memory of the hideousness of his face was so vivid that she looked around the yard in sudden fear. Could that man have had anything to do with the horrible thing that had happened to Miles? Was he, in other and very exact words, Miles's assailant?

But Miles didn't know him. Or, if he did, he had said he didn't. Suddenly she remembered that Miles hadn't even looked at the man, not even when he thanked him

for the return of the cigarettes. Of course, the man hadn't
returned Miles's cigarettes. He had *switched packages!*
She should have told Mr. Bagnall about that. Maybe it
had some connection with the happenings of the night.

Gregg slipped stealthily through the back door and
tiptoed to the car. He stuck his head inside and whispered:

"Don't start the engine, honey. Don't turn on the lights.
I'm going to push you out of here to the street. Can you
guide it backward?"

"Sure. Go ahead and push!"

She took the wheel. Silently the car rolled into the
street. She stopped it and Gregg got in.

The street sloped gently and Gregg let the car coast
into the middle of the next block before he turned on the
lights and started the motor.

"Gregg, I forgot to tell Mr. Bagnall something. In fact,
I didn't even think of it until you two had gone into the
house," Ginger began.

"Yes?"

"It's about something that happened at the theater tonight. It may have some connection with this, and yet,
I may be entirely wrong about it. Anyway, it happened."

Now that she had decided to tell it, the incident sounded trivial.

But Gregg's quick curiosity gave her courage to go on.

"Listen, honey, nothing's trivial in cases like this. What
happened?" he asked.

She told him about the ugly little man and the incident

of the exchanged cigarette packages.

"It fits right into the picture," Gregg declared with mounting enthusiasm. "Don't you see? Miles was passing something on to that strange man through the medium of a package of cigarettes. It was all prearranged."

"But what could he pass on in a little package like that?"

"I don't know that. I'm guessing the truth, Ginger, but this is my hunch. This week at Spurlock they went into production on the secret insert of the Spurlock bombsight. It's a little key that fits inside the main mechanism. It's so arranged that, when a plane gets into trouble in battle, the operator simply pushes a little lever that releases a spring and that spring blows the secret key out through the top of the plane. In that way the enemy never finds the whole bombsight, even if a plane should land intact in enemy territory. Attached to the key when it leaves the ship is a tiny bomb that explodes when it touches the ground and mangles the key, which is made of a soft metal. Usually the explosion buries it deep in the ground. Now, that key is pretty important to the enemy. Do you begin to understand?"

Ginger's mind was working like a trip-hammer.

"That key was designed in Mr. Bagnall's department and Miles works in Mr. Bagnall's department. That would mean that Miles . . ."

"Sh!" Gregg warned. "We mustn't even think about it, much less talk about it. It's one explanation, that's all, and the most obvious one. J. B. probably knows. But wait!

There's something wrong in our deductions. . . ."

"That's what I was thinking," Ginger interrupted. "If Miles were handing out some valuable information to somebody, why would they want to kill him afterward? Because, of course, they did try to kill him. I think they went away, believing he was dead, and he came to, somewhere."

"You're right!" Gregg said. "That's exactly what I think. He came to and drove the car himself. Miles was evidently trying to get to the hotel. . ."

"And Mr. Bagnall lives at the hotel," Ginger said quickly.

"And there we are!" Gregg said. "If Miles was trying to get to Mr. Bagnall, then all our deductions are wrong. We know J. B. isn't selling out the country."

"And Mr. Bagnall was honestly concerned about Miles. He didn't act as if he thought Miles was a criminal, did he?" Ginger asked.

"No, but you never know what J. B.'s thinking, or what he's planning," Gregg explained. "He never tells anyone anything. He just gives orders and you follow them blindly. Now, after I take you home, I've got to go back there and tell him about the cigarettes and the ugly man. I think he should know, don't you?"

"I think he should know right away. He might be able to interpret it. And, while it was a very *little* thing, I can't help but think it has something to do with all this." Ginger was becoming more convinced of it as they talked.

"By the way, darling, where do you live?" Gregg asked

On the Way Home They Talked Over the Recent Events

with a little laugh.

"Oh!" Ginger had forgotten that she was going home. "Go on out Sunset to San Vicente and I'll show you from there. It's a little street you wouldn't know about, even if I told you. Nobody ever does."

"Just show me the way," Gregg smiled. "Then you won't ever have to explain to anybody else again— which'll save wear and tear."

They laughed. Spontaneously Ginger moved nearer to him and linked an arm through his. Gregg looked down at her with a triumphant little laugh. The mood lasted only a moment, but it forged a little more strongly the invisible bond that was tightening itself about them.

They drove along in silence for a while, thrilled with the joy of being together, warmed by their very nearness to each other.

Finally Ginger's thoughts drifted back to the unusual events of the hours just past.

"I guess we wouldn't make such good detectives, you and I," she said smiling.

"Oh, I don't know," Gregg countered. "A good detective obeys orders and we've certainly been obeying them to the letter. Even a professional operative can rarely fit all the pieces of a case together, as they do in mystery stories and detective novels, for he never has *all* the pieces. He never does anything on his own, for—if he did—he'd probably jam up the big boss's plans. And a good detective never asks What or Why. He only asks Where and When." He looked down at her. "Which reminds me, young woman, you're a darned good person to have along at a time like tonight. You've not asked a question yet."

"It isn't because I haven't wanted to," Ginger replied, laughing. "Still, things happened so fast, I was doing well to catch my breath."

"It sure was a workout, and no fooling," he smiled. "Here, put that thing around your shoulders. It's coolish in here."

"I can't," Ginger answered, "It's—well, it's all messy. Anyway, I'm nearly home. You turn left at the next corner, then to your right and down a block."

Gregg made the turn. "I'll take that cloak back with me. J. B. will want to have it cleaned for you."

"It doesn't matter," Ginger answered.

"Yes, it does matter," Gregg insisted. "You don't want to be called upon to explain to a cleaner that those stains are human blood and instruct him just how to remove them, do you? He'd think you murdered somebody. J. B. will know just what to do with it."

"All right, then," Ginger consented. "Our house is the second on the right."

"So soon?" Gregg asked regretfully.

He pulled up and stopped.

While he walked around the car to help her out, Ginger wadded the scarlet cloak into a ball and put it on the projecting shelf below the rear-view window. Then they walked to the front porch, arm in arm.

The house was dark and the quiet little street was in deep slumber, guarded by a white and setting moon. The smell of eucalyptus filled the dew-drenched air and roof tops gleamed and sparkled, wet with dew. Soundlessly they moved through the stillness, their feet making no noise on the boarded porch.

At the door, without a word, Gregg gently took Ginger in his arms. Tenderly he kissed her, just once.

"Baby face," he whispered, as he held her close, looking down into her moonlit eyes. "I adore you."

Ginger liked his kiss—it seemed so natural and right.

"I'll talk to you tonight," Gregg whispered and was gone.

For the first time in her life, Ginger Rogers knew she was in love.

With dreamy eyes and a happy heart, Ginger watched him go. Then she put her key quietly into the lock and slowly entered the house. As her eyes became accustomed to the deeper gloom within, she came face to face with her mother standing before her in nightdress, robe and slippers.

"Why, Mother, you startled me!" she exclaimed.

"You startled me, too," Mary replied shortly. "That was Gregg Phillips, wasn't it?"

Ginger heard the angry tone in Mary's voice. "Yes, Mother, that was Gregg Phillips."

"Do you mind explaining how you happened to leave this house with one man and to return with another, a man I have asked you not to go out with?"

"I'm sorry, Mother."

"And will you further explain why you come home

at this hour and without a wrap?"

Ginger's heart sank. In a flash she realized that she dared not explain to Mary. She must not betray the confidence of Mr. Bagnall and Gregg, even to her mother. Still some explanation was due Mary. After all, she had a mother's interest and a mother's claim. Ginger felt that she would heartily approve, if she knew the truth. It seemed to her that anyone would approve. But she dared not tell Mary the entire truth.

In her desire to be fair with her mother and *yet* to hold inviolate the secret which did not belong to her, her actions—and her confusion in choosing her words—gave the impression that she was evading the truth.

"Please, Mother," Ginger said gently.

She started past Mary toward her own bedroom door. She wanted time to think.

Mary seized her arm and swung her around. Ginger could see in the half-light that Mary's lips were trembling and that she meant to have an answer.

"Mother, don't you trust me?" Her voice was low and pleading.

"I always have, but I seem to have been wrong, judging by what I've just seen."

So Mary had watched Gregg kiss her as they said goodnight on the porch! Ginger's eyes dropped before her mother's cold scrutiny.

"You will explain all this to me, young woman. As long as you live under my roof, you'll do as I say."

The cold determination of those words dissipated

Mary's anger. Her emotion was spent, and she was trembling inside. As she looked at her beloved daughter, she suddenly awakened to the realization that Ginger was not living "under my roof." In reality, it was the other way round. Mary burst into helpless tears and fled to her room, forgetting that love and loyalty would influence Ginger far more than anything else in the world.

In that moment the positions of mother and daughter were reversed. Ginger wanted to follow the suffering Mary, to take her in her arms and quiet her raging fears. But she *must* have time to think. She must face the problem squarely and be fair to everyone. So she went to her own room and quickly slipped out of her clothes and into her nightdress.

Gregg was the thorn in her mother's heart. There was no doubt about that. Did that mean that, intuitively, Mary had sensed the danger of their falling in love? But Mary didn't know Gregg. She couldn't dislike him personally. So it could only mean that Mary would fight anyone who threatened to take Ginger away. Anyone, that is, except Jimmy Daley. Why? It was so unreasonable.

Ginger picked up the brush and ran it through her hair. Suddenly in the quiet of the house, she heard Mary's sobs. It wasn't fair! Mary must not be left so wretchedly unhappy. Turning out the light, she padded softly to her mother's bedside.

Mary turned and held out her arms and Ginger crept into them. They had had their first disagreement, their first important misunderstanding. Now they clung to each other in the darkness, together again at last.

"Mommie, may I talk to you?" Ginger asked after a moment.

Mary held her closer for an answer.

"You mustn't ever doubt me," Ginger said softly. "I would never do anything to hurt you."

"I know it, Ginger. In my heart, I know it. It's just—" Mary's tears choked off her words.

Ginger said, "It's just that you're afraid for me. You want the best for me in life, always, and you're afraid something might happen to destroy that and send me off down a wrong road. Isn't that it?"

"Yes."

Ginger held her mother close and spoke tenderly, soothingly. "What's happened to your faith, Mommie? I can remember all those years when you lived on it and taught me to live on it. 'God has nothing but good for us' you said. Well, has He changed His mind about us— or about me?"

"No," Mary answered softly.

"I thank God every day for giving me you for a mother. You are so kind, so courageous, so good and so understanding. Just look back over our lives. People said we were struggling to get along, but we weren't, were we? It wasn't a struggle. We were cared for every moment, and that was because of your understanding. You were untrained to take on the job of raising a child and making the living, but you did it. I've always thought of you as 'the belle of the ball' everywhere you went. Maybe you were spoiled a little by the attention of all the young men about you, even to your sisters' beaux. You had everything your heart desired, without thinking how it came. Then, suddenly, when you found yourself faced by necessity, you squared back your shoulders, lifted your proud little chin, prayed for guidance and asked no quarter of anybody."

Mary held her child closer. Ginger's unstinted praise, her thoughts, which she had never before put into words, were like water to a thirsty traveler. Mary's weeping ceased. She felt strong and confident. Her child was grown and, what was more gratifying, her child was sound. The fear in her heart was stilled, as Ginger talked.

"We've just not been grateful enough lately," Ginger said emphatically. "That's what's the matter with us."

"I haven't been, I know that," Mary admitted.

"It's not only you, Mommie. It's both of us. We've been too busy about our silly little affairs to be grateful for all our blessings. That's why we're all mixed up." Ginger thought a moment, then went on, "What a thing for two people like us to do! Both of us know that gratitude opens the way to joy, yet here we are. . . .!"

She laughed. Mary laughed. The tension was broken. Their hearts were filled with gratitude and joy and happiness again.

Then Ginger said. "Now, Mommie, I want to tell you as much as I can about tonight. There are some things about it I cannot explain fully yet, so you must take them on faith."

"What do you mean, you cannot tell me?" Mary asked.

"Because it's a secret and it's not *my* secret. Do you understand?"

"Well .... Go on."

"Miles was injured tonight, maybe fatally," Ginger said quietly.

"An automobile accident?"

"No, not an accident," Ginger answered. "And the rest I can't tell you. But I'll tell you this much, so you won't worry. I'm not mixed up in it anyway. I've been with Mr. Bagnall, the designing engineer for Spurlock Aircraft, and Gregg Phillips most of the evening. Miles works for Mr. Bagnall at Spurlock. Now do you see why I must not talk about what happened?"

"Yes, a little. I suppose it has something to do with the country being at war and our aircraft. But—were you with Miles when he was hurt?"

"No, I wasn't. I told you, Mommie dear, I am not mixed up in it at all. But I mustn't talk about it. And you must never speak to anyone about Miles, not one word. You're to forget I told you a thing. I've told you this much because I couldn't let you guess or wonder about me."

"But how did you happen to be with Gregg Phillips, the one man I've told you I—?"

"That's the part of it I can't tell you, Mommie." Ginger hesitated a moment; then, "But there is one other thing I *can* tell you, and I think I should. I'm in love with Gregg Phillips!"

"Ginger!"

It was a wounded, hurt cry from the depths of Mary's troubled heart.

"Mother, why do you dislike him so? He's really a wonderful boy." Ginger was pleading, but Mary was hardly listening. "And he loves me, too. He told me so tonight."

Mary lashed out bitterly, "What would *he* know about love, the love of a girl like you? Men like Gregg Phillips are spoiled rascals. They run after every pretty face they see, for the thrill of it. They've had so much in their lives that everything has lost its value. He's too young to be vicious about it yet, but he'll get that way."

She paused to catch her breath.

"Even marriage wouldn't stop it. Women run after men like Gregg Phillips, even after they are married, and tear everything apart that gets in their way. Ginger, no man is so great a fool as a spoiled rich man. He never learns that it is his money that attracts designing women. He always thinks it's himself. He would destroy you, everything good about you, and he shall not do it! I shall not let him do it!"

Startled by her mother's vehemence, Ginger could say nothing. Her surprise was complete. It left her wavering and wondering. Still she had to defend Gregg, even from her mother.

"You've no right to say that, Mommie. Not about Gregg. There are people—and there are people. Not everyone would be that way. Surely there are some nice rich

"Ginger!" Mary Cried in a Wounded Voice

men in the world."

"But they are not the ones who hang around working girls," Mary flared in answer. "They stay to their own kind. You are not going to see this Gregg Phillips again! Do you understand that, Ginger? You are not to see him again!"

"Oh, Mother darling, you're all mixed up. What are you afraid of? Why is it such a crime that I love Gregg Phillips and he loves me? If you would just give me some reasonable reason."

Ginger was pleading earnestly, seriously.

Mary looked long at her child. How was she to answer a plea like that? How could she explain the anxiety in her heart? Again Mary Rogers experienced that appalling sense of inadequacy. She was not equal to such a problem. It was all so easy when Ginger was young and needed only food and clothing and kindness. Now she needed a guiding hand, wise and patient, and Mary felt herself deficient in both qualities.

At the beginning of her angry flurry, Mary had turned on the bedside light. Now she wished she were in the dark again. She knew she was being unfair. She hated herself for it. Why should it be that she could find strength only in the fury of anger? Now, as she looked into the clear eyes of this daughter, to whom she, herself, had taught coolness and straight thinking, she knew that she was losing something—she realized sadly that she was creating in Ginger's mind a doubt about herself, that, by her own actions, she was proving to her child the weakness of her own teachings.

It was a perilous thing for a mother to do. Oh, why couldn't she tell Ginger the truth? Why did she hesitate? Ginger was a grown woman now. Why shouldn't she know about the man who was her father?

But the words wouldn't come out. Mary couldn't tell her. It would win her point and show Ginger that there was a real reason for her stand against a man like Gregg Phillips. But it would also place a burden upon Ginger's heart, the burden of a dead, but never-to-be forgotten, past.

Mary had carried that burden alone all these years, never sharing the load. She had felt very proud of that. Even now, in her temptation to justify herself to her child, it seemed like treachery to do it at such a cost. She wouldn't do it! She couldn't! Bitter tears of blank despair started to Mary's eyes. She reached for the cord and pulled out the light. She crumpled back into the bed, as though to hide herself. Uncontrollable sobs shook her helplessly.

But Mary could not hide from her straightforward daughter. Ginger had watched the play of emotions, suffering, indecision and despair, across her mother's face and she sensed Mary's inward battle. Now she gathered her mother's shaking body into her arms.

"Mommie dear, you have some reason you're not telling me and I respect that," she said gently. "Believe me, dearest, I know you. You've never been unfair in your life and I was a beast to accuse you of it."

Mary gratefully patted the arm that held her and

Ginger went on:

"Nothing in life is final, Mommie. You told me that. So it isn't as if we had to settle my whole life tonight. We've all the time in the world. And we still know that God leads and guides and points to the good way for us always, don't we? So let's forget about it all for now and get some sleep. And you stop that crying. Nothing's going to happen tomorrow, or the next day, and nothing but good is ever going to happen. Right?"

"Right!" Mary answered through her sobs.

As they snuggled together, joined again in purpose, Ginger soon knew that Mary was asleep.

CHAPTER EIGHT

AN EXCHANGE OF INFORMATION

But sleep did not come at once to Ginger. In the dark stillness, the events of the evening and the night began to repeat themselves in review. What strange things could happen in an eight-hour period in a person's life, she thought.

She found that, in thinking over it all, she was glad, more glad than she could say, that she had been a part of it, for in no other way could she have found Gregg. She said "found" to herself because, while she had known him now for several summer months, she had not *really* known him. Now she did, and he knew her. How could it ever have been managed otherwise?

Then she thought of Miles, the man with whom she had started out so matter-of-factly to a première. What sort of a man was Miles, anyway? Could it be that he was a traitor to his country? He is French, she said to herself, and now France is involved with helping Germany—at least, part of it is. To which part did Miles belong? She wondered if Madame DeLhut would know. She remembered Madame's serious, *"Who is Miles Harrington?"* that night in her office. That was the night Madame handed her the scarlet cloak. . . .

"The *scarlet cloak!*" Ginger exclaimed, almost aloud,

and every muscle in her body sprang to attention. "The *scarlet cloak!* Miles wanted me to wear it! He talked Mother into letting me. He *insisted!*"

Then, as her agile mind traced the events of the evening, a thought struck her and she sat straight up in bed.

"That's it! The scarlet cloak was *the signal!* It didn't matter who wore it. It could have been any girl. Some message was to pass from Miles to someone who was told to look for a man accompanying a girl in a scarlet opera cloak!"

That was why the ugly man had watched her and looked at her as though she should know him. He was evidently trying to identify himself to her, not knowing that she was innocently unaware of their scheming and plotting.

However, that would mean that Miles did not know or care who was to receive the message. He had had his instructions from somewhere and was following them to the letter. He had dropped the cigarettes purposely. She had known that at the time, really. That was why he had tried to turn the conversation, when she had wanted to tell him about it. He hadn't wanted her to see it or interpret it. It had been cleverly arranged—it was only by chance that she had seen it.

Mr. Bagnall must know about this. She glanced at the illuminated timepiece on her mother's dresser. It was after three o'clock. She wondered if Mr. Bagnall would be back at the hotel. Should she try to reach him and tell him?

But earlier in the evening Mr. Bagnall had vetoed the use of the telephone. It wouldn't be safe to tell him over the telephone, because it would take lengthy explaining to make him understand. She'd have to tell him in person. He should know at once, though. How and where could she reach him? She could call Gregg—he would know.

With her thoughts racing like unleashed hounds on a scent, she was becoming fidgety and jumpy. She wondered if she could manage to get to her own room without waking Mary. Mary, sound asleep, had no consciousness of Ginger's gentle movements to extricate herself from the covers or her departure from the room.

Softly Ginger closed her mother's bedroom door. As she passed, she looked through the living-room door and saw the telephone. It seemed to beckon her to do something *now*. She wondered if Patsy were still on duty at the hotel. Should she try? If she went to her room and fell asleep, half the day would be gone, maybe more, before Mary would wake her. If she stayed awake the rest of the night, she would have to do her calling before her mother wakened in the morning.

She went into the living room and closed the door gently behind her. She dialed the hotel.

Patsy's sleepy voice answered:

"Seaview Arms. Good *morning*."

Ginger almost whispered, "Patsy, listen. It's Ginger."

"Well, as if I wouldn't know it. But what in the world are you doing up this late? Did you go to the première?"

"I'll tell you all about that tomorrow. I can't talk much now," Ginger murmured. "You must do something for me, Patsy."

Patsy was instantly all ears and attention.

"Sure, kid. What is it? What's the matter?"

"Call Gregg Phillips' room and see if he's in. If he is there, tell him that I must see Mr. Bagnall the first thing in the morning—that I've found out *something more.* He'll understand. But don't let him call me back. Understand?"

"I get it!" Patsy's normal efficiency was wide awake, but her curiosity was very nearly getting the best of her. "You don't want to talk to him even now, is that it?"

"Yes. Don't connect him. And don't let him talk you into it."

Patsy said, "Can you hold the phone while I ring?"

"Yes. But, if I should hang up suddenly, don't ring back, will you?"

"Okay, Ginger. I'll leave the key open, if you want to listen to what he says."

Then she repeated for Ginger what she was to tell Gregg and rang his room.

Gregg answered at once. Ginger could tell that he had not been asleep, that he had probably just got in. Patsy gave him Ginger's message.

"When did she call you?" he asked Patsy.

"Just—well, just now," Patsy answered.

"I'd better talk to her. Will you ring her back?" Gregg asked.

"I've strict orders from her not to ring her back," Patsy answered.

"Then how are you going to give her my answer?" Gregg persisted, as Ginger had known he would.

That stumped Patsy for a moment. Then, "I've got my ways of getting messages to her without ringing her house and waking up her mother and all the neighbors," she said.

"I get it," Gregg answered, accepting the verdict. "Well, let's see now . . . the first thing in the morning . . ." He was thinking out loud. "Tell her I'll pick her up at eight o'clock and, in the meantime, I'll make a date with J. B. for her and take her directly to him. How's that?"

Ginger was thinking fast as she listened. Eight o'clock, here at her own house! Well, she'd have to do it, even though it would pain her mother. But maybe Mary would still be asleep. Anyway, there wasn't time to argue the point. So, while Patsy hesitated, wondering what to answer, Ginger whispered to her, "Okay."

Patsy heard it—and so did Gregg.

"What did you say, Patsy?" he asked.

"I said 'Okay'," Patsy answered quickly, then asked, "Do you want me to ring Mr. Bagnall's room for you, Mr. Phillips?"

"No, Patsy, thanks. But you can tell my girl, when you talk to her, that I still adore her, even more than ever."

"How much is that?" Patsy could not forego the temptation.

"She knows and, for your own information, Miss Nosey,

you're speaking of the future Mrs. Gregg Phillips. That is, if she's crazy enough to take on a zany like me."

Patsy's heart swelled with romantic tenderness and thrill.

"Oh, Mr. Phillips, I hope she does! I think it would be wonderful—just wonderful!"

Ginger, listening, had the odd feeling of an eavesdropper. Gregg had not said as much to her, yet here she was, being proposed to by proxy, as it were.

Then she heard Gregg saying, "Then you're in my corner? Good! Just for that, you can call me by my first name. And, by the way, will I have much opposition from mother and dad? I mean, what will they think about it?"

"Ginger doesn't have a dad," Patsy revealed. "But her mother is the sweetest woman. You'll make a hit with her, I'm sure."

Patsy was well acquainted with Mary's antipathy to rich young men, but, in her exuberance, she was quite certain this one would be different.

"I hope so," Gregg answered. "Well, good night, and don't forget."

"I won't," Patsy answered. "Good night—Gregg."

Ginger heard Gregg hang up.

Then Patsy said, "Are you still there, Ginger?"

"Yes."

"Then you heard him. Oh, gee! Isn't he swell? Are you the lucky girl, Ginger! And he don't care who knows it, either. That's what I like about him. You're going to be right where you belong, with yachts and mink coats and ermines. Gee, I can hardly wait! But, you see, that's like me—always a bridesmaid and never a bride. Gee, I wonder when I'm gonna find me a fella, too."

As Patsy paused to catch her breath, Ginger whispered, "Patsy, I'll talk to you tomorrow. I've got to go now."

But Patsy didn't take that seriously. "By the way, Maggie's leaving us."

Margaret Paine was the operator whose shift followed that of Ginger and Patsy on the Seaview Arms switchboard. Margaret—"Maggie" to the girls—held down those last dawn hours alone, from three o'clock in the morning until the day operators came on at seven. Ginger liked her very much, the little she had known her. Maggie was pleasant and obliging, but dissatisfied with the hours of her work. It was not surprising that she had succeeded in getting what was probably a better job—or better hours, at least. But it was of interest to Ginger, for it meant that some other girl would come in each morning as she and Patsy were ready to leave.

"She is?" Ginger whispered.

"Yeah." Patsy had to tell the whole story. "She's got a swell job with one of those juke-box switchboards, the kind that plays the records you ask for from the cocktail bars. You know."

"That's wonderful," Ginger said. "Tell her I'm happy for her. See you tonight."

To keep Patsy from launching into some other subject, Ginger unceremoniously hung up.

Back in her own room, Ginger turned on the light and

selected the clothes she would wear in the morning. She laid them out carefully, then put a pencil and paper on the dresser. If Mary were not awake when she was ready to go, she would leave a note.

She tiptoed into the kitchen and brought back the alarm clock. She set it for seven-fifteen and put it under her pillow. At last she slipped into bed and turned out the light. But she could not sleep. She was tired, but there was so much to think about.

Gregg!

What was she going to tell Mr. Bagnall about the scarlet opera cloak? It was all very plain about the cloak. She was sure now that it had been Miles who had sent it to her in that anonymous way. She reviewed his conversation on the telephone. He had led her into talking about it and, unsuspicious, she had fallen in with his plan. Then Miles was a—why, he was a Fifth Columnist!

The next thing she knew the alarm clock was ringing and it was seven-fifteen. Quickly she turned it off and listened, wide-awake. Her highly attuned ears, accustomed to the sounds of the house, heard no stirring or movement within it.

Mary was still sleeping. Maybe it was better that way.

Gregg came exactly at eight. Ginger did not allow him to ring the doorbell. She was waiting for him on the porch. As she saw his car approaching, she ran down the walk.

Gregg looked sleepy-eyed, as though he had just awakened. As he held the door open for her, he said in the

Ginger Slipped into Bed and Turned out the Light

middle of a yawn:

"Heavens above us! You look as fresh as a daisy. How dare you?"

Gregg explained that he had arranged with Mr. Bagnall for the three of them to have breakfast at Sardi's. The idea appealed to Ginger. A public restaurant would be the best place to meet. No suspicion could be attached to their being there. It would look purely social, a breakfast date. In her inexperience in such matters, she did not know that, with men like Mr. Bagnall and Gregg, more important business is often transacted over public dining tables than in offices.

Mr. Bagnall was waiting in one of the little booths against the wall. The headwaiter led them directly to him. He had already drunk his orange juice.

"Had to have it," he explained.

Ginger could see that he had not been in bed at all. His face was haggard and lined and ashen pale. He was worried, but he tried to hide it under a faint, forced smile whenever they spoke to him.

Breakfasters filled the room. Late arrivals joined parties as Ginger and Gregg had done. They gave the waiter their orders. Ginger decided to wait until Mr. Bagnall broached the subject before she told him the reason for their meeting there.

After the waiter brought their fruit course, Gregg spoke to Mr. Bagnall.

"How's Harrington?"

"We can't tell yet," Mr. Bagnall said, his brow furrowed. "The doctor says it's concussion. He hasn't regained consciousness for even a moment."

Then his whole face changed. A smile took the place of the frown. Gregg might have asked him about the weather, for all his expression showed.

Ginger glanced at Gregg. He too was smiling affably, as though their conversation were only pleasant chatter. Their behavior was a cue for her own actions.

So when Mr. Bagnall turned to her and asked in a low voice, "You've found out something else, Ginger?" she smiled before she answered.

"It isn't that I've found out something. It is something I think you should know, something that I feel is connected with the other things you know."

Then, with conversational pauses and misleading smiles—for the doubtful benefit of anyone watching—she told the two men her explanation of the riddle of the scarlet cloak and her suspicions of Miles's connection with it. As she went on with her story, she saw Mr. Bagnall and Gregg exchange glances. But it was impossible for her to know just what those looks meant. They certainly were not surprised. She had a distinct feeling that she was telling them something which they already knew and that they were trying to decide how to deal with the fact that she knew more than she should.

There was no comment from them as she finished her story.

After a pause, in which he kept his eyes on his plate, evidently carefully framing what he would say to her,

Mr. Bagnall thanked her. Then, he said:

"I know it is not necessary to tell you that you must never mention a word of all this to anyone. And, believe me, I am grateful that you have not asked questions which I cannot answer. All this is very important, Ginger. It is all-important to our government and to the winning of the war. More than this, I cannot tell you. Unwittingly, you have joined up, as it were, and you will have to remember that a good soldier never asks questions, never talks about orders, goes where he's told to go and reports only to his superior."

Ginger said, "I've told my mother nothing, except that Miles was hurt last night. It explained why I came home with Gregg, instead of Miles. And I asked Mother to mention that to no one. She won't."

Mr. Bagnall thought about that a moment.

"I can understand why you had to explain your strange actions to your mother."

"It is the only reason I told her even that much," Ginger answered and Mr. Bagnall looked pleased.

Again there was a long pause during which Mr. Bagnall seemed to be planning. Finally he said:

"I hope this is the end of your experience in this matter, Ginger. But I cannot promise you that it is. I may need your help—or—"

He hesitated.

"You know I'm more than willing to do anything I can, Mr. Bagnall," Ginger said.

"I know that," he smiled. "And I'm grateful, but—"

Again he seemed to be unable to put into words what he wanted to say.

Ginger's eyes were wide in her eager desire to know. Mr. Bagnall, quite solemn now, looked directly at her. "There are some things in this matter that I cannot control," he said. "You may be dragged into it again in some way I cannot now forsee. So I can only ask that you keep in close touch with me and, if you cannot find me, with Gregg. If anything happens to you, anything that is unusual, tell one of us."

"I will," she answered eagerly.

"Keep your suspicions alive," Mr. Bagnall admonished. "You know what I mean. I wish very much that I could be more explicit with you, Ginger, but I cannot."

"I know," she answered sympathetically.

"And I wish I knew how to warn you. But it is impossible to anticipate the form in which it might be presented to you again. So you'll have to keep a sharp eye and an alert suspicion."

Gregg said, smiling mischievously, "It will be entirely to my liking that you should keep very close track of me. You know, just in case."

They laughed together and Mr. Bagnall rose to take his departure.

"We'll hope you'll have no need to call on either of us," he said.

"Kill-joy!" Gregg exclaimed, when Mr. Bagnall was gone and the two were alone.

As Ginger watched Mr. Bagnall walk through the front

door of the restaurant, she felt that she had played her last scene in this drama. She felt a twinge of regret, realizing that it would be a long, long time before she could ever know the riddle's true answer, or even the secret of the part she had played. It was impossible even to guess the truth through Mr. Bagnall's words or actions. No one could ever know what he was thinking. Well, it was over and she hoped that she had been of some help.

Then she became conscious of Gregg's concentrated gaze and she turned to him. His eyes were filled with the warmth of his affections for her. She could not pull her own eyes away.

"Now that I'm awake and we're alone," he said softly, "may I tell you that I think you're beautiful and wonderful and that I'm falling head-over-heels in love with you, baby face?"

"Sh!" Ginger whispered, hastily glancing around her. "We're not alone. What do you want to do, tell it to all the world?"

"I certainly do," he replied. "Hey, Alex!"

The headwaiter was standing but a few steps away and turned when he heard his name called.

"Yes, Mr. Phillips," he said, coming quickly to their table.

"May I make an announcement?" Gregg pretended that he was going to rise and make a speech then and there.

Ginger grabbed his sleeve and pulled him back into the seat.

Alex, used to all manners of jokes from his Hollywood guests, only laughed. He caught the significance of Gregg's intention and looked appraisingly and approvingly at Ginger, who blushed like a schoolgirl, in spite of herself.

"I don't blame you at all, Mr. Phillips," Alex said.

"Come on, let's go," Ginger said, rising, "You're not a safe person to be out with in public places. You're liable to do anything!"

Alex smiled with them as he followed them to the front door.

CHAPTER NINE

In the car, going homeward, Ginger's mind raced ahead to that moment, not very far off, when they would drive up in front of her house and Mary Rogers would be awake and see them. It would be another happening that she could not explain fully to her mother.

She wondered—but she heard Gregg speaking.

"You know, darling, this should be at night, with a great full moon and millions of stars. And this car should be a canoe on the bosom of a deep blue lake," he was saying. "But how can it be when you work nights and go out with other guys on your only night off? This isn't the time or the place to ask you, prosaically driving up Hollywood Boulevard with both hands on the wheel and both eyes on the road, but I can't wait. I have to know something. You see, any minute now a big, bad man might jump off a lumbering truck and carry you off. Then I'd never know. By the way, are you listening?"

"Yes, darling. I'm listening."

Gregg slammed on the brakes. The car behind smashed into their rear bumper. Gregg paid no attention to the crash.

"Hey! What did you say? What did you call me? Say that again!" he cried, looking into her eyes.

144

"Yes, darling," she repeated tenderly.

"Oh, my gosh!"

He gathered her into his arms as best he could and kissed her. Then he drew back and looked at her searchingly. In her eyes he saw his dream come true, the answer he had always dreamed of finding some day in the eyes of the one girl in all the world.

For the moment they were alone in that wide, wide world. They did not hear the horns of impatient motorists. They did not see the passers-by, who had slowed to watch them. They were conscious only of themselves and what they meant to each other.

A deep, authoritative voice startled them.

"Here, you two! Not on my street!"

The corner traffic policeman was leaning in at the window, his arms crossed over the edge of its frame.

"Go'way, Jake. You bother me," Gregg said and turned again to Ginger.

But she was aware now of the attention which they had attracted, and she colored to the roots of her hair.

"Ooo! Let's get out of here!" she exclaimed.

Lifting one of her hands to his lips and turning to the policeman, who seemed loath to leave, Gregg sang, like a little boy in the first grade, "I've got a *see*-cret! I've got a *see*-cret!"

Jake sang back, "And you're gonna get a *tic*-ket, if you don't get *go*-ing."

He stepped away, waving his arms. With not a car in front of them for blocks, Gregg drove rapidly away.

"Oh, gee, honey, you mean it, don't you? You're not kidding, are you?" Gregg asked a little later.

Ginger wondered at the humility, the depths of hope, from which this plea had come. The joking, frivolous Gregg, whom she had known before, was gone. His words were filled with a deep sincerity and tenderness. Ginger felt that, for the first time, she was seeing the real Gregg Phillips.

When she did not answer at once, he pulled up to the curb and stopped. They were in the residential district of the older part of Hollywood, on a tree-arched, narrow lane that led over the brow of a hill and ended in a canyon.

There was fear in his eyes as he turned, waiting for her answer, fear of her possible answer in the negative.

She studied his face. She knew that this was the one man in all the world for her—to bring her happiness.

Then she smiled. "I mean it, darling. I love you."

He didn't move. He just sat looking at her. He hardly breathed. The moment was heavy with the weight of its future. Like a runner who drops from sheer exhaustion, after reaching the tape first, Gregg closed his eyes. Then he ran a hand through his hair, and Ginger saw the trembling of his fingers. He took a long breath. Then he reached over, took her hand and reverently kissed it.

"You'll never be sorry, your whole life long," he said softly. "And you're mine! I can't believe it yet." Suddenly his whole manner changed and a light of purpose came over his face. "Look, sweetheart, let's get married this

Ginger Smiled. "I Mean It, Darling. I Love You."

minute."

Ginger watched him, loving every changing expression on his handsome face.

"But we can't, Gregg. Not in California. We have to wait three days, you know."

"Then let's start this minute for some place where we don't have to wait. What do you say?"

Ginger grew serious.

"Gregg, wait. That part has to come later. I want to, believe me, right this minute, but—"

She hesitated.

"Come home with me, will you?" she finally said.

"Sure!" He started the car. "I should do a little announcing around among my family, too, I guess. But, Ginger, promise me it won't be long. We won't wait very long, will we?"

"I don't want to wait. But come home with me now and let's talk to Mother."

There were days to come that would fill Ginger with deepest regret for that decision. Days would follow when she would wish from the very bottom of her soul that she had followed the madness of Gregg's wish and had rushed away to marriage with him. It is upon such unpredictable circumstances that sometimes lives are wrecked or happiness sacrificed.

Together they walked up the steps of the neat little cottage. Both dreaded the coming interview. Gregg was smiling, trying to seem as nonchalant and gay as he could, and Ginger was steeling her courage to the making of a frank announcement. She had no intention of warning Gregg of the ordeal they might face because, in the calm light of morning, her mother might have reconsidered. It was only right to give her that chance and, if she had, to avoid any unpleasantness which might hang over the future relationship of the mother she adored and the man she loved.

Between the two she could have no choice. She had made her decision to marry Gregg Phillips and her mother was—her mother. Now the two must find their own meeting ground without her assistance or suggestion.

Mary was not in the living room when they entered and Ginger could not hear her anywhere in the house. Gregg looked about him and smiled. The neatness and good taste of the small room surprised and pleased him. Inexpensive but good prints hung on its walls. Dainty, tasteful lamp shades, probably made by Mrs. Rogers, were colorfully placed in just the right spots beside gaily upholstered chairs and divans. The colors of the room, he could see, had been chosen by an artistic eye. He thought that he had never seen so much accomplished with so little expenditure.

"Sit down, Gregg, and I'll find Mother," Ginger said hospitably.

"Just a moment." He detained her by taking her in his arms. "Tell me just once more that it's really true, that you're mine, all mine."

"It's really true, darling."

He kissed her and held her close, wanting never to let

her go.

Then they heard the back door close and they knew that Mary was coming in.

Ginger called, "Mother, will you come here?"

"Is that you, dear?" Mary answered and entered the room.

"Mother, this is Gregg Phillips. Gregg, my mother," Ginger introduced them.

Mary had frozen on the spot.

"How do you do?" she said formally.

"It's very nice to know you, Mrs. Rogers," Gregg said, and flashed her a nervous smile.

Mary instantly decided that Ginger had told the young man that he was not welcome here and that he had brazened out this meeting, in spite of Ginger's warning.

Watching her mother, Ginger saw her misconception of Gregg's attitude and sprang to his rescue. She stood beside Gregg, linked her arm through his and faced Mary.

"Mother, we have something we want to discuss with you," she said. Then she turned to Gregg and asked, "Haven't we, dear?"

"I should say we have," Gregg answered emphatically, laughing. "Something pretty important, too, I should say. We wanted to talk it over with you, since you're going to be involved in it, Mrs. Rogers."

Mary's thin lips tightened into a straight line, hardening her pretty mouth.

"I shall never be involved in anything that will concern you, Mr. Phillips, and we might as well understand each other at the outset," she stated harshly.

"Mother!"

Ginger's pathetic cry was heavy with disappointment. She saw that Mary was not going to give Gregg even a fighting chance, that she meant to end the interview as speedily and definitely as she could.

Mary pretended not to hear. She still talked to Gregg.

"My daughter told me last night that she was in love with you, Mr. Phillips, and I forbade her to see you again. This morning she defied me. Now I shall put it squarely up to you. You are not to see my daughter again or communicate with her in any way. Is that clear?"

Gregg was stunned for a moment. Then he rallied. His shoulders went back, his chin shot forward. He did not flinch as he said:

"I'm sorry, Mrs. Rogers, but I can make no such promise to you. In the first place, you have no right to demand it without explaining *why* you do it. By any chance, have I ever done you or Ginger an injury?"

"I do not think it necessary to explain my motives to you, Mr. Phillips. I demand that you do not see Ginger again."

She spoke with a determination to dominate this situation which had arisen contrary to her expressed wishes.

"Then I shall have to defy you, too," Gregg answered, with equal determination. "Ginger and I love each other and we are going to be married just as soon as we can arrange it. Nobody in the world can keep me away from her."

"Oh, please!" Ginger interrupted. "Let's not say things we will regret."

Nothing is final, she kept saying to herself. Nothing bad is ever final!

"Gregg," she said aloud, "come out here with me."

She led him toward the front door, for she could see that Mary would not weaken.

Unresisting, Gregg went with her. He turned at the door, trying desperately to find something to say to end properly the strange interview. But he could not find the right words so, silently, he went with Ginger. Ginger closed the door after them. She led the way to the car and Gregg felt that she was asking him to leave. He bit back the rush of resentment which swept like a torrent to his lips seeking voice.

At the car he turned.

"What does this mean to us, Ginger?" he demanded.

"I wish I knew," she answered sadly. "I can't understand why Mother acts like this."

"You knew it last night."

Gregg was hurt—his tone revealed it.

"Yes. Mother told me I was not to see you again, just as she told you."

"Then why didn't you tell me? Why didn't you prepare me for what I was going to meet? You let me walk right into it. Do you think that was fair?"

"Oh, Gregg!" She was near to tears. "I'm beyond knowing what's fair and what isn't. I had hoped that, when Mother met you, she'd change her mind. I felt that maybe you, yourself, could straighten her out. Don't you see, darling, I wanted to give you both a clear field?"

"But what, in Heaven's name, has she got against me? What have I done?"

"Nothing, darling. Nothing."

"This is asinine!" Gregg exclaimed in complete exasperation. "Your mother's just plain crazy!"

"Please, Gregg, don't say things like that," Ginger pleaded, "about—my mother."

"Well, did she give you any reason for her hating me? Or is this a sample of mother-love?" Gregg was being sarcastic in his disappointment.

"Yes, she gave me a reason. It has very little to do with you, personally. You wouldn't believe it. It sounds so silly to you and me. But it seems to mean so very much to Mother."

"Well, are we going to begin by having secrets from each other? Tell me, Ginger."

She made two attempts before she brought it out.

"It's because you're rich!" she exclaimed at last.

The words rocked Gregg back on his heels. He had expected almost anything but this. He gasped. He couldn't understand it. His agile mind leaped here and there, trying to find an explanation.

All he could say was, "Well, that's a new one!"

They did not look at each other. For a long moment neither spoke.

Then Gregg said, "Of course, I'm *not* rich. I work for

a living. Whatever we have, as a family, belongs to my father and mother. They're both in darned good health, thank Heaven, and it will be a long day before any of it comes to me, if it ever does." Then his impatience broke its bonds. "But what does that have to do with you and me? Your mother's either plumb crazy or she's a— a—I don't know what!"

Hot tears flooded Ginger's eyes.

"Oh, darling, she's so unhappy. She hates herself, really, for doing this. Believe me, Gregg, she's a wonderful woman. Someday you'll know that. She just thinks you're rich and spoiled and will make me unhappy."

That made some sense to Gregg.

"Oh, is that it? You mean, it's as simple as that?" he asked, a ray of hope shining in his eyes. He squeezed her arm tenderly. "Maybe I've got your mother all wrong. But she's got to give me a chance to prove it."

They were silent, thinking. Ginger hoped that, by some miracle, Gregg could work it out. Gregg wondered how to go about solving the problem which faced them.

Finally Gregg said, "A while ago you said you didn't know what this was going to mean to us. Why did you say that, Ginger?"

"I don't know why I said it, Gregg. I'm baffled."

"Could you stop loving me?"

She looked squarely into his eyes. "No."

"Then, could you sacrifice us, our future, over this, your mother's ridiculous idea?"

Gregg was very serious and Ginger could see how much

"Oh, Darling, She's So Unhappy," Ginger Said

weight her answer was going to carry. She hesitated and that hesitation discouraged Gregg.

"No," she said finally.

But Gregg could not accept it as a full denial. He knew that she had made some mental reservation and he could not bridge it. He opened the door of the car and got in.

"When you make up your mind definitely, will you let me know?"

He started the car.

"Gregg, I said 'No,' " she pleaded, watching him helplessly.

"But you didn't quite mean it, Ginger." His coldness chilled her heart. "I'll call you tonight."

But the smile he flashed to her was not open or happy. He drove away, leaving her standing at the curb.

One hour ago she had been happily engaged to be married to the man she loved. Now that happiness had known the blight of tears and the bite of sarcasm. She stood between two fires of emotion. Disaster awaited her whichever way she might turn.

She went directly to her room to think it out and, mercifully, fell asleep.

Mary wakened her when her dinner was ready. They did not refer to the scene of the morning. In fact, they talked very little, and that little was strained and unnatural. Finally Ginger went to the hotel to her job.

But Gregg had not been so fortunate. No sooner had he turned the corner at the end of the block than he regretted his impulsive departure. He had acted like a spoiled child and he suddenly realized that his actions supported Mary's contention. He wanted to go back, but he had so many things to do that had already been left too long undone.

He could still hear Ginger's voice pleading, *"Gregg, I said 'no.'"* It was his one ray of hope, for, by leaving abruptly, he had left the field wide open to the influence of the unreasonable woman who was Ginger's mother. In his heart of hearts he knew that Ginger had not changed. But could Mary's pressure change her? He squirmed inside of his own helplessness.

CHAPTER TEN

THE MYSTERIOUS MR. DUNLOP

All that day Gregg had an uncontrollable desire to call Ginger at her home. But he remembered the unpleasant scene of the morning in that house and he gave up the idea, marveling the while at his allowing anything to deter him from his usual straight road to any goal.

But when his watch said it was seven o'clock that evening he called the hotel from a pay-station. He wanted to talk to Ginger the moment she arrived at her switchboard.

Patsy answered his ring. Ginger had not come in yet, she said, though she expected her any moment.

Patsy was busy. The day girls had left the moment she had come on duty. But, busy or not busy, Patsy could not restrain her curiosity. She had to talk.

"I told her what you said last night—that is—" She paused, suddenly remembering that she hadn't told Ginger because Ginger had been listening. "That is, this morning. But there was no comment from the fair lady. Oh!" Patsy interrupted herself hastily. "Just a moment. Here's another call. Don't go 'way."

Gregg was in no mood to listen to Patsy's chatter. He had an impulse to hang up. But he couldn't do that. He'd started the whole thing, himself, and how could

Patsy know all that had happened in the meantime? Also, Ginger might come in while he waited.

Patsy came back on the wire. "It seems you're not the only one that wants to talk to Ginger. This is the third call in the last twenty minutes. Pretty popular, that gal!" Patsy wanted it to sound like rivalry, just for the interest it might generate.

But Gregg did not rise to the bait. "When she comes in, will you tell her I'll call her again in ten minutes? She should be there then, shouldn't she?"

"Well!" Patsy said to herself, when he was gone. "What's the matter with him?"

When Gregg called back ten minutes later, Patsy told him that, unusual as it was, Ginger had not yet arrived. It was twenty minutes past seven and Ginger had never been this late before. She didn't know what to make of it.

"Surely she'll get here in the next five or ten minutes," she added.

But Gregg couldn't call again for an hour or two, he said. Would Patsy please tell Ginger he would call the first moment he could get to a telephone? Patsy would, of course—she was *glad* to do it!

When five more minutes had ticked themselves away across the face of the big clock set in the wall above her head, Patsy began to worry. Something must have happened! If she called the house and Ginger had left there on time, Mrs. Rogers would be worried, too. That wouldn't do! By all the rules she should call the front office and report to Mr. Dudley. But nobody in Patsy's circle ever "snitched on a pal," if she could help it.

When five more minutes were gone the way of the other twenty-five, Patsy was fit to be tied. She was dialing wrong numbers and mixing up her board like a beginner. She was torn between worry and irritation. Of all the nights for Ginger to choose to be late! Cards were coming up from the desk downstairs like mad. They had to be set into the racks. People were moving out. Rooms were vacated. New guests were being registered and those alphabetic racks were never easy to do, even when you weren't worried sick and "busy as all get out."

Gee, why was it that people began calling on the telephone, and getting calls, the moment their luggage was set down in a hotel room? Calls came in for names you never heard, before their cards were sent upstairs from the desk! You had twice as much work on such a call, because you had to ring the desk and check before you knew what room to ring.

It seemed to Patsy, as she sat there alone, that every old guest had moved out of the hotel and every room had a new tenant. "Mr. George Diggens, please." George Diggens? Now who in the world was he? Probably one of the new aircraft workers. Yes, a call downstairs told her she'd find him in 911.

"Harold Cripes? Cripes, did you say? Just a moment." Another one! Yes, he lived here, too.

They went to bed early, these aircraft workers. For the first time in a year she sat with the "call board" almost in her lap. "Call Mr. Wales, Room 614, at five o'clock!"

Patsy had never heard of Mr. Wales and five o'clock in the morning at Seaview Arms had always meant a fishing date before. Now this Mr. Wales wanted her to make the call permanent, except on Sunday!

Where was that tardy Ginger?

A glance at the clock told Patsy that something was definitely out of order—the routine of Ginger's life was severely strained, if not broken altogether. Patsy's exasperation changed to real worry. Something had to be done about it. She couldn't get Gregg. Anyway, he wouldn't know. She mustn't call Mrs. Rogers—yet. There was Jimmy Daley! But she didn't know Jimmy Daley. Still, he'd be the most logical one. She scanned the huge telephone book as she answered calls and worked her board. Finally she found the number that seemed most likely to be the right Daley. The address was near Ginger's own.

It was the right number. "Oh, hello," Jimmy said, when he came to the telephone. "I've heard Ginger speak of you so often I feel I know you."

But Patsy soon changed his gay tone. When she finished talking, she had Jimmy's promise to get in his old car and follow the bus route to the hotel, keeping a sharp lookout. But first he was to go by the Rogers' house and, under some pretext, learn whether Ginger had left. When he reached the hotel, he was to come up to the telephone room and report to her.

Patsy had just disconnected her call to Jimmy, when

Ginger rushed into the room. She was out of breath. Without a word of explanation, except a brief, "I'm sorry, Pat," she literally threw her hat across the room, neatly depositing it on the table under the window, climbed upon her stool, donned her head-piece without regard for her hair, switched on her board and began taking calls.

Quickly Patsy dialed the Daley number again, but there was no answer. She knew Jimmy had left on his fruitless errand.

"What in the world happened?" Patsy asked.

Ginger did not answer. She found her board busy enough to give her an excuse to evade Patsy's direct question. She hadn't yet decided how to explain. It had to be handled neatly. That required more thought and more preparation than she had had time to give it.

There was no doubt in Ginger's mind that the experience, which she had just had, meant something other than had appeared on the face of it. She could think of nothing else as automatically she handled her calls, dialed numbers and ran practiced fingers through the pile of register cards still unracked before her. But what could it mean? There was just the possibility that she was only imagining any meaning in it at all. Still she couldn't overcome that intuitive certainty that had been growing on her for the last half hour. That man had been pumping her for information! Yet he had handled it all so carefully.

When she reached the corner near her home and saw

no bus, she had sat down on the long iron bench provided for waiting passengers. If only she had kept her eyes open. Then, if Mr. Dunlop had really planned to pick her up there, she would have noticed his car standing down the street and would have seen it move to pull up in front of her. Then she would have known! As it was, she had to give him the benefit of the doubt, for, when she first saw him, he was apparently swerving from the line of traffic over to the curb.

Mr. Dunlop was smiling broadly, as he stopped his car, and his bright little eyes sparkled with what seemed to her to be surprise and pleasure at seeing her.

"Imagine my good fortune to find you on your way to work, and that way the same as mine," he had said.

At the time those words had meant to her exactly what they said. But, as she reviewed the episode now, they could have been rehearsed. How did he *know* that she was on her way to work? But, she thought reasonably, anyone who knew her at all would know she was on her way to work at that time in the evening.

He had held the car door open invitingly and, while she remembered having had a sensation of hesitation, she had smiled and stepped in.

She had found herself unable to match his effusive gaiety. His odd phrasing of his sentences kept her busy, trying to figure them out. The right moment for an answer had always passed before complete understanding had reached her. He seemed never to say anything spontaneously. He sounded like a radio announcer, reading a prepared script. The sunny day, the weather, the flowers and the sunset, all came under his scholastic observation, with here and there a poetic allusion, always accompanied by a very knowing and patronizing smile, as if he were hoping she appreciated the privilege of consorting with such a brilliant mind. He himself seemed most highly appreciative of it. Sometimes she felt very silly, giving him a quick, set smile that kept leaping out before he had time to figure out just what he was talking about.

When, finally, they had reached the turn, where the boulevard meets Palisades, he had looked at his watch.

"We've made splendid time!" he exclaimed. "And I'm glad, because it will give me the opportunity of showing you a house I'm considering buying. It's just a short way from here." He had not said, "by your leave," or asked if she'd care to see the house. He had simply passed the intersection and sped on, turning in the opposite direction from the hotel at the next street.

Ginger had half-heartedly objected by looking at her watch and mumbling, "I have to be on time at the hotel."

But he had waived her objection aside with, "It won't delay you at all."

Then he had stopped the car in the driveway of a large house, far back from the winding street and hidden behind a leafy screen of bushes, flowers, and stone walls.

"You really cannot get a perspective of it from here. Supposing we walk to the front. Architecturally it is not

"Supposing We Walk to the Front," Mr. Dunlop Said

a pure specimen, but it is very comfortable inside," he had said.

Although she mumbled another objection, Ginger had walked with him to the front of the house. She had no idea why she did so, but his manner was so persuasive and gently domineering that there seemed no way to combat it without taking open issue, and she had lacked the courage to do that.

She could find nothing to say about the house. She knew nothing of architecture. She was unfamiliar with houses containing more than five rooms. Mentally she stumbled after him, confused and never able to catch up with him.

"I have the keys. Let's peek inside. I'm sure you'll like it," he had said finally.

Those words aroused her courage to voice objection.

"I'm so sorry. I can't. You see, I've only a few minutes more and I must go to work," she said firmly. "Maybe some other time . . . " And she started walking toward the car.

Mr. Dunlop hung back. For a moment she thought that he was going to be annoyingly persistent. Then, with a shrug of his shoulders, he walked on with her. He opened the car door and helped her in. He seemed to be taking his time, disregarding her need to hurry.

Before he meshed the gears, he looked at her smilingly and said, "You were at the première last night and you looked very lovely. I saw you. I was there, too."

"Were you?" It was all Ginger could think of to say.

"You went to the Mocambo afterward, didn't you?"

"Yes, I did." She smiled and looked at him.

From the expression on his face, he seemed to be waiting for her to add something to her short remark. Suddenly all the important happenings of the past twenty-four hours flooded over her. The lethargy in which she had been wrapped, waiting until she could get away from this man and go up to her switchboard where she belonged, left her. Her agile mind snapped awake. Mentally she put up her guards. She turned away a moment so that he might not see the change which had come over her.

Still he did not start the car. "The young man you were with?" he asked, leaving the query in mid-air, as though encouraging her to take up from there and finish it for him.

"Yes?"

Mr. Dunlop was quick. She could say that for him. "I've always liked him," he said, completely altering his tone. "I've known Miles for quite a while, you know."

"Oh, really?" As she spoke, she wondered if all this could be purely coincidental, could mean nothing. Still, she must remain on guard.

"Yes. In fact, we've been very close for some time. He was to have had luncheon with me today, but, for some reason, he didn't show up," Mr. Dunlop continued.

She flashed him a disarming smile. "I haven't known him so very long. Is he in a habit of doing that to his friends?"

"No. That's what makes it so peculiar. He's a very conscientious fellow. It isn't at all like him. I thought he might have mentioned something to you last night, something he had to do today that would explain. . . ."

Pretty clever, Ginger thought to herself. Instead of answering at once, she looked at her watch. "Goodness, it's after seven! Do you mind driving me on? I must get to work. I'm a working girl, you know."

Obligingly he started the car and wheeled out of the mansion yard into the main drive, headed toward the hotel. But Mr. Dunlop had no intention of dropping the subject where she'd so dexterously left it.

"Miles said nothing to you about today, then?" he asked.

"No, he didn't."

"Probably you were out pretty late." He waited. When she did not immediately answer, he said, "He is a splendid dancer, isn't he?"

"Oh, no, you don't!" she said to him mentally. Then, aloud, "I don't know that I'd be much of a judge." Suddenly deciding to give him no further chance to pursue the subject of Miles, she added, "You've known Madame DuLhut for a long time, too, haven't you?"

"Yes, for years. I knew her husband in Paris. Leon DuLhut was one of the greatest hotel men of his time, of any time. I stopped with him off and on for more than ten years. I've lived abroad most of my life, you know."

"But you are American, aren't you?" If she kept him talking about himself two more minutes, they would be at the hotel.

"Yes, by birth. I was born in New York. But, Europe, my dear, is the place for real living! Americans know nothing about living. They simply exist. Of course, with the war. . . ."

Ginger couldn't help saying, "Yes, with the war it was safer to come home to mother."

"Now, my dear, you are behaving like every American. Provincial!" His tone was indulgent.

Then they were drawing up to the motor door of the hotel and their little battle of words was over. To avoid any chance of prolonging the conversation, Ginger bounded unceremoniously out of the car and hurried toward the door.

But Mr. Dunlop called to her. She stopped.

"If Miles should call you today, will you tell him to get in touch with me? It is really most important," he said.

"I'll tell him. And thanks for the ride." She smiled and rushed into the hotel.

Too impatient to wait for an elevator, she had run up the stairs. The clock in the motor court had told her she was already thirty-five minutes late. But it wasn't the lateness that caused her wild hurry. It was an almost frantic urge to get away from Mr. Dunlop. Shivering, she had felt as if she had suddenly seen a snake, all coiled and ready to strike. And, while she was wise enough to keep beyond its striking range, it was still an unpleasant sight to see.

But getting away from Mr. Dunlop did not bring relief or forgetfulness. Lurking in the back of her mind was the persistent conviction that Mr. Dunlop had followed a well-prepared design in asking her those questions about Miles, that his passing the bus-stop at just that time, and his picking her up to bring her to work, was the result of careful planning.

Why? That was the stickler! Why?

Strange and unexplained things had happened to Miles. Did this man have any connection with them? If so, why should he have to ask her? Oh, she wouldn't put it past him. Like Patsy, she could say with full conviction that she didn't like him. Patsy was pretty sound in some of her snap judgments. But where did Mr. Dunlop fit into the picture?

After her talk with Mr. Bagnall there was no longer any doubt in her mind that what had happened to Miles was the work of saboteurs. It was not clear to her on which side Miles belonged. But she'd bet her next summer's hat that Mr. Dunlop had some interest in it, somewhere, and that he was trying to find out what she knew, or if she knew anything. Pumping her, that's what he had been doing! Well, he didn't get anything out of her. Or did he? Maybe her very actions spoke louder than words could have done. Anyway, she'd know soon enough, for, if he were interested and her deductions were right, he'd try again. She decided to leave the road open to him to try again, if he liked.

Should she tell Mr. Bagnall or Gregg about this? When she asked herself that question all her faith in the importance of the episode crumbled. They'd probably listen politely and smile to themselves and make her feel like a child playing at cops and robbers. But if, in the end, it should prove important and she hadn't told them! She must run the risk of their smiles and indulgence and tell them.

"What I want to know is, where *were* you?" Patsy's voice broke into her thoughts. "Everybody in the world almost has been calling for you. Gregg Phillips called twice and he'll call you again as soon as he can. But where were you?"

Ginger hadn't had time to prepare an answer sufficiently plausible and yet not untruthful to satisfy Patsy's curiosity.

"I went on an errand," she said and was saved from further explanation by a call from a guest. That call kept her busy for a few minutes and gave Patsy time to forget to pursue the subject.

While Ginger was busy with the call, she was conscious of a commotion behind her, of Patsy leaving her board and opening the telephone room door, but she didn't turn around until her own board was clear. Then she turned and looked at the one person in the world whom she would never have expected to see, Jimmy Daley.

"Jimmy! What are you doing here?" Ginger's words didn't sound hospitable, but Jimmy understood.

"I called him," Patsy explained quickly. "I was worried about you."

"That was very sweet of you both," Ginger said. "Maybe I'd better introduce you two formally." So she introduced them, watching Patsy's blushing loss of composure and Jimmy's unconcealed flustration. The eyes of her two friends were locked, while they stammered and grinned at each other, for the moment forgetting her very presence. Ginger smiled, remembering Patsy's denunciations of Jimmy before this meeting. She was laughing inwardly, when her board recalled her to duty.

"Patsy, hadn't you better step outside in the hall with Jimmy? You know the rules," she said.

As she turned to her board and Patsy opened the door, Ginger saw a man standing just outside the door and heard Patsy talking to him. When she had completed the call, she turned to see the man standing inside the telephone room, evidently waiting for her to finish.

"I'm from the telephone company," he said, smiling.

Ginger saw an official badge pinned to the breast of his coveralls. In his hand he carried a little black leather bag, containing his testing instruments.

"Oh," Ginger said, "They must have called you before I came on duty."

She turned back to the board to look for the ticket which would certainly be there, reporting such a call made by the chief of the day force.

She found no ticket.

"I'm sure I can't say what you were called for," she said finally, in a tone of dismissal. "There isn't a call-ticket here."

The man referred to his own block of report tickets.

"It says here, 'Hotel Seaview Arms, Room 953, bells don't ring,'" he told her. "Probably some trouble in the box in that room. It was filed at 3:30 this afternoon."

Ginger didn't need to refer to her alphabetical house list to know that 953 was the suite just vacated by Mr. Dunlop, but she did run her finger down the house rack, then thumbed through the sheaf of unracked cards on her board.

"I guess it will be all right for you to go up and fix it," she said. "There's nobody in that suite now. But this kind of work should have been done in the daytime, you know, when the chief is here. I'll have to get front office permission."

There was nothing extremely unusual about the incident. Such things are part of the routine of telephone switchboards. But Ginger's brow was furrowed as she rang downstairs. The night manager answered. After a moment of hesitation, he okayed the procedure.

"We have to pick up these calls as we can nowadays," the telephone repair man explained. "So many of our men are enlisting, the rest of us have to work night and day. Been on duty thirteen hours today, myself. Goin' home right after this, though, you bet."

He started toward the door.

"Just a moment," Ginger detained him. "I'm going to make out a ticket since there is none here. What's your badge number?"

"397."

She looked at the badge—"397" was correct.

"I'll have a maid let you in the suite. Call me when you're finished, will you?"

"Sure will."

When he was gone, Ginger began to worry about the incident. She didn't feel just right about it.

"Now wait!" she admonished herself. "Are you going to begin suspecting everything and everybody? You're getting jumpy."

But, she thought, who wouldn't be after all that had happened to *her?*

A light came up on her board. It was from Madame DuLhut's penthouse on the roof. It was Madame herself. Ginger experienced again that little-girl thrill of joy when Madame said, "ZheeZhee, are you veree beesy?"

"No, Madame, we're not. In fact, it's slow tonight."

"Zen have Patsy take ovaire. Come to my apartment, ZheeZhee. Yes?"

"Oh, yes, Madame," Ginger answered, and all her worries were lost in pleasurable anticipation of the visit with Madame.

She turned to call Patsy from the hall. Then she remembered—Madame knew where she had gone last night. How could she answer the questions Madame would ask and yet tell nothing?

And the scarlet cloak! Madame would surely ask about that.

It was unnatural for Ginger to lie. In her rather uneventful life she had never resorted to the little white lies which other girls often thought it necessary to tell. It did

"ZheeZhee, Are You Veree Beesy?" Madame Asked

not occur to her to make up a story for Madame. Instead, she tried to decide how much she could say without telling anything, and without having to announce that she could tell nothing, as she had done with her mother.

Her desire to go to Madame's suite turned to reluctance and she moved slowly toward the door. She wished that she did not have to talk to anyone until this strange business, into which she had been plunged, was finished.

Jimmy was bidding Patsy goodnight as Ginger opened the door. She thanked him again for his trouble in coming to find her and returned to the room with Patsy in tow.

Ginger saw that Patsy's cheeks were rosy and that her eyes were filled with a new and glowing light. For the moment it made her forget her own troubles.

"Why didn't you tell me he was that nice?" Patsy asked, knowing that she could not hide her feelings from Ginger.

"I did, but you wouldn't listen," Ginger reminded her.

"Wouldn't I?"

"No, you wouldn't. You insisted he was not the kind of man I should marry. Remember?" Ginger smiled when she saw the quick, apprehensive look that crossed Patsy's face. "Now you know how wrong you were," she added. "Jimmy's just about the nicest boy in the world and I'm glad you've changed your mind about him."

Enjoying Patsy's confusion, and without giving her time to answer, Ginger went on, "Madame wants me to come to her apartment, so you're to take over. I'll be back soon. Be a good girl."

She turned toward the door, but Patsy stopped her.

"Do you mean you're going to marry him, Ginger?" Patsy's doleful, comical expression proved to Ginger that Patsy was more than just interested in her school pal, Jimmy.

"Of course not, silly!" Ginger's hand was on the door knob and she flashed Patsy a smile of assurance. She couldn't leave her in doubt.

"He asked me for a date on my day off," Patsy said. "That is, if you—"

"If I don't mind," Ginger finished for her. "You go along and have a date. You'll like Jimmy better the more you know him." She left the door and came close to Patsy, who had climbed back upon her stool. "As for me, I'm going to marry the man I love."

Patsy's eyes fairly popped out of her head. "You mean Gregg Phillips?"

"I don't mean anyone else."

And Ginger was gone.

As she went down the hall she heard, through the telephone room's closed door, the high, shrill, feminine squeal of her overjoyed switchboard partner. She could imagine Patsy fairly kicking the front panel out of the floor board in her unruly, unleashed emotion. It sent her up in the elevator with a warm and generous feeling toward her homely little friend, who had found appreciation, at last, in the eyes of a good boy.

CHAPTER ELEVEN

"Now, come and tell me all about eet," Madame said, as she led Ginger onto the balcony overlooking the rear gardens of the hotel.

It was warm and comfortable in this sky room, which was glass enclosed and heated for nighttime, while it served Madame as a sun porch in the midday. Ginger had always loved this balcony room, with its blue chintz chaisé longué and chairs, its hanging baskets of rare vines, its colorful pottery wall brackets and red-tiled floor, dotted with deep blue rag rugs, each one outlined with a pure white fringe.

It was definitely Madame's room and she fitted into it like a hand into a French glove. And, when she was in the room, she always wore a gown that blended perfectly with its coloring. As she looked at the little French woman, Ginger wondered if Madame's evenings spent in this room were planned and dressed for.

In a white wire basket on the low table between their chairs were two tall glasses of a lemon-fruit drink, tinkling with ice and garnished with fresh mint. Madame handed one of them to Ginger.

"You had a fine time last night, yes?"

"Yes, I did, Madame. I went to so many places I'd

never seen before."

"ZheeZhee, tell me, what deed you wear?"

"I haven't any clothes—I mean, what *you* would call clothes, Madame." Ginger was a little girl again, sitting at the feet of this woman who knew all about fashions and clothes. "I wore just a cheap little evening affair of black lace, and not very good lace, I'm afraid."

"You must not say so, ZheeZhee. You—weeth zat figure—you make a lettle five-dollar dress look like a French model. On you anysing look good. And you wear over zat dress zee scarlet cloak? Yes?"

Ginger felt her eyes shift before the bright, friendly question in the eyes of the older woman. "Yes, I wore it. Mother didn't want me to at first but Miles—"

She had spoken the name without thinking. She, herself, had brought the forbidden subject into their conversation.

"Miles—ees he zee boy you go weeth?"

"Yes." Ginger added nothing to the short answer.

"Thees Miles—you like heem, maybe?"

"Oh, I—"

"No, you don't like heem. Zat I see. Zen you have not so good fun last night. Deed you go dancing?"

"We went to the Mocambo." The answer would do, if Madame did not press her inquiries further.

But Madame had no intention of giving up. She leaned forward in her chair, anxiously scanning Ginger's face.

"He deed not dance so good and he brought you home early, yes?"

Ginger's eyes glanced downward, away from Madame's gaze. She was commandeering all her wits to keep away from subjects which she did not wish to discuss. She looked up. Madame's intent gaze startled her. The older woman's eyes demanded an answer. Her smile had suddenly vanished.

The trite reply, which Ginger had half formed, died on her lips. She stammered and stuttered:

"Well—I—we—that is—Miles—"

"What happened?" Madame asked anxiously. She seemed to be holding her breath, waiting for Ginger's reply.

The truth trembled on Ginger's lips. She wanted to blurt it out and have it over. But, just in time, she remembered Mr. Bagnall's warning and her promise. Not even Madame, as much as she loved her, could be trusted with what she knew.

She dropped her eyes. "I—I can't tell you, Madame," she said haltingly.

There was an awkward silence. Then Madame, her whole manner suddenly changing, said:

"I should not be asking you zees sings. Come, Zhee-Zhee, we must laugh. We get so serious. Nosing so awful have happen to you. You all togezzer in a bunch. Eef he ees not zee nice boy, you just do not go out weeth heem again. Eet weel geeve heem a lesson. Maybe he call you today and apologize?"

It was a clever switch of manner, but it left Ginger unconvinced. Madame had wanted to know something about *Miles,* had wanted desperately to know! Why? Ginger had the same feeling she had had when Mr. Dunlop had pressed her for information. Only, with Madame, there was not, in her heart, that same feeling of resentment. In fact, she had only narrowly escaped telling Madame all about it. She had really wanted to tell her.

She had been sharp and witty with Mr. Dunlop. She could practice no such artificiality with Madame. She didn't want to. So, in answer to Madame's last remark, she looked down at her fingernails and simply smiled.

"But you feel veree fine, wearing zee beautiful cloak, ZheeZhee?" Madame was herself again—friendly, not anxious.

"I loved wearing it. Everybody looked at me. I knew they were looking at the cloak."

The moment of tension had passed, and, strangely enough, the very subject which she had most dreaded before coming up to Madame's balcony, the scarlet cloak, had brought the relief.

"One day I shall geeve a beautiful party and you shall come and wear eet. And I shall invite Gregg Pheeleeps to come and see you een eet, too."

Madame's eyes twinkled mischievously with the matchmaker's gleam.

Ginger had to bite her tongue to keep from telling Madame that Gregg had already seen her in the cloak. Instead, she said, "Madame, I'm going to marry Gregg Phillips."

A thunderbolt could not have rendered Madame more

speechless. She gasped, "ZheeZhee!" Her happiness at the
news, expressed in that one exclamation, was not feigned.
"Darling, tell me all about zees. When deed eet happen?"

"Last night."

Instantly Ginger knew that she had caught herself in a
trap which she herself had set and sprung. She was
frightened. There was no backing away. Madame's elastic mind had snapped at the bit of information and she
was making no attempt to hide the fact that she had
stumbled upon knowledge for which she had been
angling.

"Last night?"

There was an entire volume of questions wrapped up
in those two small words.

"Yes, last night."

Ginger's words were like a confession. Why should
everything important in her life be inextricably tied up
with those few unhappy hours of that night?

"You must tell me about zees," Madame said slowly,
seriously, almost pathetically.

She had uttered almost the same words a few moments
before, but then she had spoken with a twinkle in her old
eyes, thrilled with curiosity and humor. Now her words
were heavy with a desperate need to know something
Ginger knew.

What was it Madame must know? Why should she
want to know *anything* about the happenings of last
night which were so unrelated to her?

Until that moment Ginger had not thought of suspecting Madame of interest in the dark side of the night's happenings. But now she was shocked to find herself tabulating the facts. Madame was French! Miles was French! France had capitulated, at least politically—had gone over to the enemy! It could be! If Madame were sympathetic toward Germany instead of toward the Fighting French, *it could be!*

How dare she even think of such a thing? Ginger jumped to her feet and walked to the window. The thought was too horrible to bear calmly.

Madame followed her, coming to her side and just standing there, her whole attitude one desperate interrogation point.

There was no longer any pretense between the two. Madame's guards were down. Whatever it was she wanted to know, she must know, at any cost. The once-twinkling eyes were brimming with unshed tears. Ginger, startled and troubled, knew that there was nothing to do but face the issue squarely. She was trapped, helpless.

"ZheeZhee, you must tell me—I must know!"

Madame's lips trembled and her mouth was downdrawn at the corners. She laid an affectionate, pleading hand on Ginger's shoulder. The hand was shaking.

Choking back a sob of sympathy, Ginger answered, "Madame, please . . . . I—I cannot tell you—anything."

It was as if she had slapped the older woman. Slowly Madame's hand dropped away from Ginger's shoulder and her whole body sagged forward, as though she were fainting. Ginger reached out for her as she swayed. But, brushing away the girl's hand, Madame stumbled to a chair and sank into it, sobbing and covering her face to hide her grief and desperation.

Instantly Ginger knelt beside her. "Madame, please don't. What is so wrong? What are you afraid of? What is it you want to know?" The questions tumbled over each other.

Without answering, the older woman arose and walked away, as if she were trying to escape from whatever Ginger might have told her in her sympathy, if Madame had pressed her. She did not look at her again.

"Forgive me—darling, forgive me," Madame sobbed. "We must talk no more. You must go. *You must go!*"

It was beyond Ginger's understanding. Slowly she started toward the living-room door. In the apartment a telephone bell clanged sharply. Ginger stopped. The buzzer over the balcony door sounded. Madame made no movement toward the telephone on a little table close to her favorite chair. So Ginger answered it.

"Yes?"

It was Patsy. Gregg was calling Ginger.

Then Gregg's voice spoke. Ginger told him where she was. He noticed the strained tone in her voice.

"What's the matter, darling?" he asked.

"I'm with Madame. She—she doesn't feel so well—she—"

"You haven't told her anything, have you?" There was quick worry in his voice.

"No."

"I don't know why I asked you. I know you wouldn't."
But Ginger knew that he was relieved. He went on, "I'm
going to pick you up tonight and take you home, honey."

"But, Gregg, it will be so late. You need sleep."

"I have something pretty important to talk to you
about. Anyway, I want to see you. I'll wait in the motor
court. If I'm asleep in the car, just turn the hose on me."

It was good to hear a little humor in his voice. It was
good to know she would see him tonight.

"All right, Gregg," she answered, caressingly. "And I'm
glad."

She hung up. Madame had not moved from the window, though she was no longer weeping. Her back was
toward Ginger and the girl knew that Madame was still
suffering. She could not go without making some effort
to restore to the older woman some of her former peace
of mind, even though she felt that, in her pain, Madame
would rather be alone.

"Madame, if you really want me to go, I will, though
there was something I wanted to talk to you about," Ginger said, still standing by the telephone.

It was a master stroke to relieve the tension, and Madame turned toward her from the window. The tears were
gone from her eyes, but they were red and swollen and
the lines about them had deepened. There was no resentment in Madame's face. Instead she smiled a thin,
sad smile of understanding.

"Yes, darling, what ees eet?" she asked.

"I wanted to ask you about Mr. Dunlop," Ginger said,

encouraged. "Who is he?"

There was a thoughtful silence, as Madame moved slowly to the wing-back chair and sat down. Finally she said:

"Zabel Dunlop—who ees he? Why, I know heem een France many years ago. I deed not know heem so veree well, but he come and go een our hotel zere. I nevaire know anysing he ees doing . . business, I mean. My husband deed not like heem. Zabel ees veree bad spoilt and veree selfish man. He was nevaire married, zat I know."

"Is he an American, Madame?"

"I have always thought so, but he leeve mostly abroad for years. He was always traveling somewhere—but pretty soon he was back."

Suddenly Madame's eyes grew wide and she leaned forward, searching Ginger's face. The peace which she had regained was gone.

"Why do you ask me zees, ZheeZhee? . . . What are you thinking about Zabel Dunlop?" she asked anxiously.

Ginger managed to hold on to her matter-of-fact tone.

"Oh, I was just curious, I guess. I feel as your husband did. I don't like him."

It was plain that Madame was not convinced, but she seemed to realize that it was useless to press Ginger for any further explanation. Once again tears filled her eyes. Bravely she tried to hide her emotion.

When she spoke her voice was controlled.

"I deed not know you knew heem, ZheeZhee," she

said quietly.

Ginger hesitated for only a brief moment. Then she explained:

"I met him one afternoon as I was coming to work. My hat blew off. He picked it up. He's called me regularly for a long time and I've been doing some little telephone errands for him."

"*Telephone* errands?" Madame's face grew grave.

"I've called his house in New York for him and his summer home in Florida and a few other places, that's all. Just routine."

"What do you mean, hees house een New York?" Madame's eyes were sharp and questioning.

"He wanted me to tell his butler to put in some sugar. I called his gardener in Florida to tell him to move a tree from the front yard to the back yard. I made the calls according to his directions."

Madame did not speak. Ginger could fairly hear the wheels going round and round behind those gimlet eyes. Then Madame rose and started toward a coat closet in which, Ginger knew, she had a direct telephone line. That telephone was not serviced through the hotel switchboard.

As she moved, she said, "You must go down now, ZheeZhee. Goodbye. I weel call you later."

That was a dismissal. There was no doubt about it. It left Ginger with a flat feeling—she hardly knew what to do. Obediently she started toward the outer door. She could hear Madame dialing the telephone in the closet.

Before she closed the door behind her, Ginger heard
Madame say hurriedly, excitedly, "Rogers. Tell heem I
must see heem at once. You must get heem, please."

Now, what could that mean? Ginger's feet scuffed the
carpet as she moved down the hall toward the elevator.
Her thoughts were so busy that she was not even conscious of walking. She must gather her wits together and
begin at the beginning.

At first, she remembered, Madame had been only so-
cially curious about her good time last night. She had
asked about Miles, but she had stumbled over his name.
So she knew nothing about that part of the story.

Ginger recalled that once before Madame had asked,
"Who is Miles Harrington?" That was the night Madame had given Ginger the scarlet cloak.

Madame had asked about the scarlet cloak tonight, but
they had passed over that subject without difficulties. It
was when she learned that Ginger had seen Gregg Phillips last night that she had started to cry. Why? What
could Gregg have to do with it? Madame liked Gregg,
Ginger knew.

Suddenly Ginger wondered if Madame wanted, for
some reason, to know everything that happened last night
and if she had deliberately pretended to be merely "social-
ly curious." Had she hoped to learn what she wanted to
know without Ginger realizing that she was giving the
desired information? That was the only conclusion that
made sense. But why should Madame do that? Why
couldn't she just ask?

Ginger Wondered What Madame Had Really Wanted

Perhaps she didn't "just ask," because she was afraid of straight answers. Perhaps she was afraid that Ginger wouldn't tell her. Maybe she *knew* that Ginger wouldn't tell her, but hoped that Ginger would drop some hint from which she could draw her own conclusions. If that were true, then she did know that something important had happened last night. But she hadn't known that Gregg was in it and, when she had learned that, she had become frightened about something.

Ginger forgot to press the button on the elevator.

"O-o-oh!" she said, almost aloud, remembering Madame's exact words, *"he brought you home early, yes?"*

"And when I didn't answer right away, she first began to be so serious," Ginger recalled. *" 'What happened?' she asked, and she was scared."*

So Madame's interest was in Miles! *"ZheeZhee, you must tell me—I must know!"*

That was about Miles! That was when she cried and looked so pathetic.

At that moment Madame became, to Ginger, the connecting link between the little pieces of the puzzle. And, as she went on, mentally reviewing the scene with Madame, she realized that it had been the mention of Mr. Dunlop which had aroused Madame into action. All of this put Mr. Dunlop into the pattern of events, also, because that very afternoon, he, too, had insisted upon knowing about Miles.

So both Madame and Mr. Dunlop were aware that

something had happened to Miles. But neither could possibly have any information concerning *what* had happened. Each, in his separate way, was trying to find out. It was funny that both should have come to her. Obviously that meant that neither of them knew that the other had talked to her.

The pattern was slowly taking shape—growing clearer! Mr. Bagnall had hidden the battered Miles, and Madame and Mr. Dunlop wanted to know where he had been concealed. Miles was French—Madame was French—Mr. Dunlop was French in sympathy.

Ginger pressed the button for the elevator. She scarcely knew when it stopped for her or when she entered, so busy were her thoughts. Madame may have acted strangely, but she was also sincerely and deeply moved, as well as worried and frightened. There was nothing scheming or vicious in her curiosity. *"I must know!"* she had cried, as if desperately wounded. So it must be that man, Zabel Dunlop, who was the villain of this complicated French triangle—this three-sided puzzle.

The elevator stopped at the second floor. Ginger stepped out and walked down the hall. She unlocked the door of the telephone room and entered. Patsy was busy with a call. Ginger did not immediately go to her board. She sauntered to the window and stood, looking down on the garden below and thinking about the whole strange business.

What was the answer to the riddle of the scarlet cloak? Suddenly she noticed a figure walking under the lights from the tennis court in the garden. It was moving toward the main walk of the hotel, down the path that led only from the one bungalow in the yard, the bungalow occupied by Mr. Dunlop.

With a start of surprise, Ginger recognized the figure—it was the telephone repair man. What was he doing down there?

She watched. The man walked down the garden path and, without coming through the hotel, went on to the main driveway. He entered a small car, parked in the motor court, and drove away.

Ginger frowned. What could the repair man be doing there? He was supposed to go to Mr. Dunlop's old suite, not to his bungalow. The front office had not given an okay for him to go to the bungalow.

She went to her board.

"Patsy, did that telephone repair man report back on room 953?" she asked.

"You mean the guy that was here? No. I meant to ask you what he was here for."

Ginger rang the central office. The girl in charge could find no order for the man to visit the bungalow. However, the head clerk was gone, she explained. Maybe the day clerk would know. She suggested that Ginger call again the next morning.

Ginger disconnected and began to write a report for her own day chief. Under ordinary circumstances she would have dismissed the incident without thought. But in her present frame of mind she wanted to know exactly what was going on.

Ginger meant to make sure of things, so far as she was concerned.

She called the front office and asked whether the night manager had okayed a telephone repair man to go into Mr. Dunlop's bungalow. The answer was "No." So she reported his visit and was informed that she must be mistaken, that he had probably just got lost in the grounds and was trying to find his way out.

"Why won't people wake up!" Ginger exclaimed silently. *"Don't they know we are at war? Don't they know that the enemy stalks the country?"*

Ginger could guess that, if she had voiced her suspicions to the night manager, he would think her slightly balmy, to say the least. At that moment she didn't have the courage to face his derision, to try to make him understand her alarm. Besides, how could she make her suspicions understandable to anybody?

Well, she could tell Gregg tonight. She had so much to tell Gregg tonight about Dunlop and Madame and the telephone repair man.

Indeed, there was so much to tell and yet there was nothing really definite and tangible. Everything was indefinite, intangible—that is, simply "sort of suspicious."

But it was enough to worry Ginger, and whenever she was worried she could not rest till she did something about it.

CHAPTER TWELVE

A MAN CALLED JOSH

Gregg was sound asleep in his car in the motor court when Ginger came out to keep their appointment at three o'clock that morning. He sprang into wide-awakeness when she opened the door and got in. Affectionately and tenderly he took her in his arms and kissed her. Then he started the car and they drove slowly out of the hotel grounds and onto the boulevard.

Neither spoke. In their silence, they healed the wounds of their morning parting.

They passed the clump of hedge where, but a few hours before, they had found Miles unconscious. They saw the place on the lawn where the angry man had challenged them with his cold resentment. It seemed to Ginger that these strange events had all happened ages ago. She felt so much older now, more mature in every way.

Gregg smiled, his eyes twinkling with happiness. Only a few short hours before, his life had only lightly touched her life, Ginger recalled. It thrilled her to think that, from now on, and forever, it would be *Ginger and Gregg,* linked inseparably together. She moved nearer to him and slipped her arm through his chummily.

Gregg patted her hand and whispered softly, as if he had read her thoughts, "Darling."

She sensed he had something new to tell her. It was something good, too, she knew by his manner. He kept stealing sly glances at her, glances full of his secret. She smiled back, increasingly curious, but waiting for him to choose the moment of revelation.

"I suppose I should take you somewhere to eat," he said at last. "You must be hungry. But I have something terrific I must tell you."

"What?" Ginger asked gently, only wishing to show some interest.

Gregg turned the car to the curb before a tree-lined plot of vacant land and turned to look at her when he had parked.

"I found out today that I know your father," he said quietly. "In fact, I've known him for years."

His approval of the man who was Ginger's father was evident in his voice.

"My *father?*"

"Yes. Josh Rogers. His name is really Joshua Rogers, but everyone calls him 'Josh.' He's a wonderful man! Can you imagine how happy I was when I found out that he was your father, that you were Josh's daughter? Young lady, our dads went to school together and were boyhood friends!"

Ginger heard his amazing words with an odd feeling of unreality. She had never before talked to anyone about her father. Once, when she was a little girl, her Aunt Nore, Mary's sister, had started to tell her something about her father, but Mary had come into the room and stopped it. Ginger knew nothing at all about her father and her mother's strange silence had given her the feeling that, had she known, she would have not been proud of him. Sometimes, secretly, she had wondered about her father, and that was all.

"I've never seen him," Ginger said simply.

"I know. Am *I* going to have the kick of my life, introducing you and Josh! And are *you* going to like him!"

"Introducing us! You mean—he's here?" Ginger could hardly believe her ears.

"Yep. Right here in Los Angeles. He's seen you and talked with you over the telephone. But he's never come near you on account—well, on account of your mother. Talk about the long arm of coincidence! Josh Rogers used to visit in our home when I was a little boy—and now *I'm* going to marry his daughter!"

He pulled her to him, his arm about her, and continued, "You know, there was a time when my family didn't have so much. And Josh was rich. We lived in a little house and Josh stayed at the big clubs. But he never failed to spend Christmas at our house, after his mother died —your grandmother that was."

Gregg paused, then went on reminiscently, "I remember, as a kid, I bought Josh's Christmas present out of my little allowance, just as I bought Mother's and Dad's. Josh never failed me. He always brought me the thing I wanted most. And it was always the best of its kind. Honey, that's *your dad!*"

He laughed. His feelings ran so much more deeply than he could express, as Ginger intuitively realized.

"Is—is he rich?" Ginger faltered, after a moment in which she tried to understand the significance of the amazing things which Gregg was telling.

"No, not any more. That was the funny thing. The 1929 crash made a pauper out of Josh and a rich man out of my father. In fact, I think it was Josh's business head that put my father in the way of being a rich man— pointed out the opportunity to him. We always knew there was a wife and little daughter somewhere, but it was one thing which we never discussed with Josh. I talked to Mother long distance today and told her. She's —well she's too pleased for words. She's dying to come out and meet you. She's happy I'm going to settle down and glad I'm in love and—well, everything's so swell I'm bustin' wide open with happiness."

He held her closer, and Ginger snuggled nearer.

"Here I am so full of myself I'm forgetting about the things you want to know. You're kind o' stumped, aren't you, honey? Well, fire away! Ask anything you want to know about Josh, because you're going to meet him to-morrow."

"*Tomorrow?*"

"Yep. You and I have a luncheon date with him."

"Is he—?"

"Married again? Nope. He's never been divorced from your mother. Never wanted a divorce, he says. I believe he's still in love with your mother."

"Then what happened?"

"That I don't know. But I have a theory. I worked it out from the things your mother says about me. She doesn't want you to marry me because I'm supposed to be rich and because that means I'm spoiled—mostly by women, especially fond mothers and aunts and so on. Probably that is what she thinks caused the break-up of her marriage to Josh. Understand?"

"It makes sense."

"You're going to love this Josh, Ginger, even if he is your father."

They both laughed.

Ginger tried to shake the confusion out of her head.

"I had so many things to talk to you about and now this has knocked it all out of me," she said. "Tell me, how—how does he *look?*"

"Well, you look like him from your nose up." Gregg halved her face with the side of his hand. "You have his eyes and forehead. He's over six feet. Used to play football. Handsome. He's lived a clean life, so he's younger-looking than he really is."

"What does he do?"

"He's with the Federal Bureau of Investigation. He's one of their best men. He's stationed right here in town. We lost track of Josh for a good many years. That is, we never lost complete touch with him, but we didn't see him so much after he went to Washington with the F.B.I. Then I found him here and I've seen a lot of him this last year. You know, it's funny, but Mr. Bagnall knew you were

Josh Rogers Was With the Federal Bureau of Investigation

Josh's daughter all along. I found that out today, too."

"Does Mr. Bagnall know him, too?"

"Listen, honey, everyone knows Josh Rogers. You're going to be so darned proud of him! He's mighty proud of you, too. I'll bet he won't sleep a wink tonight, waiting for luncheon tomorrow," Gregg laughed. "He was as thrilled as a kid on Christmas Eve."

"Does my mother know he's here?" Ginger asked in a very quiet voice.

"We don't know whether she does or not, but *I* think she does. It's strange that you've never seen his name in the papers."

"I wouldn't have thought anything of it, if I had. The name wouldn't have meant a thing to me. I never saw it but twice, once on my birth certificate and once, long ago, in my aunt's family album."

"It's a shame you had to miss knowing a man like Josh all these years."

They thought about that in silence for a while.

"Something dreadful must have happened," Ginger said at last and Gregg knew that she meant the something which had parted her mother and the father who, from Gregg's enthusiastic description, must be a prince among men.

They talked of inconsequentials—the kind which only sweethearts find interesting—for a few moments more; then Ginger said:

"Gregg, it's getting so late! You'll have to take me home. Mother will be worried. I didn't tell her that I was meeting you at this crazy hour of the night."

Gregg started the car.

"What were all the things you had to tell *me* about?" he asked as they drove toward her house.

"They were about Madame DuLhut, Miles Harrington, and Mr. Dunlop. I've found out—"

"You've found out *what* about Dunlop?" he demanded suddenly.

"Gregg, Mr. Dunlop is mixed up with Miles, I believe. In fact, I'm sure of it. And Madame knows something about Miles, too."

Quickly, because they had so little time left, she described the half hour which she had spent with Mr. Dunlop.

Gregg was serious and thoughtful when he said, "Probably it is only that Dunlop knows Miles and asked you about him, because he saw you with him. But I'll see Mr. Bagnall tomorrow morning and tell him, if you want me to."

"I wish you would. And Madame kept trying to get me to tell her about last night. Once she cried and said, 'I must know!' as though her heart were breaking."

"She did? That might be important."

"I know it is—otherwise why should Madame have cried?"

By this time they were at Ginger's door. She realized with a pang that she hadn't made what she knew entirely clear to Gregg, but there was no more time. She'd have to go in. And, while she had a feeling that she should stay and convince Gregg of the seriousness of the things which she had seen and heard, there was another force driving her irresistibly into the house.

Mary might be awake. She might look out and see them together. In fact, she was probably watching them now, unhappy and miserable at the sight. Ginger could not bear to cause more unhappiness to the mother whose heartache she understood better tonight than she had before.

It was her own fault, she decided somewhat guiltily, that Gregg had dismissed her news about Madame and Mr. Dunlop with merely a promise to tell Mr. Bagnall about it the next day. In her haste she had told her story incoherently.

Gregg kissed her good-night and drove away.

Mary was not awake. She had not heard Ginger come in. Ginger was glad because she wanted to think, wanted to be alone. Tomorrow she was going to meet her father! It was bewildering. It would be one of the most stirring events of her life. It was far more important to her than the other important things which had happened to her that day.

But she had a strange feeling that she should not let the meeting with her father overshadow those other happenings. Like a crazy quilt, the patches of information which she had acquired had begun to piece themselves together into a pattern. She must not allow them to become lost in her personal interests. Instinct told her that her deductions were true. Intuition told her that there was more she could learn of importance to the welfare of her country and its gigantic war effort.

As she turned out her light, she almost resented the fact that she was here, in the safety of her own home, going to bed, when there was so much work to do. She lay wide-awake in the dark, thinking.

She thought of Madame. But somehow, she could not bring herself to put her friend in the same category with the two men. Madame knew something, yes, but it was not a guilty knowledge. Of that Ginger was convinced. But she wished, nevertheless, that she knew what Madame knew.

Then, suddenly, two new patches dropped themselves onto her crazy quilt and stitched themselves permanently into place. Gregg had said that her father, Joshua Rogers, was an official of the Federal Bureau of Investigation. Madame had called someone on her private wire that night and had said, "Rogers." At the time Ginger had thought that Madame meant her. Now she knew!

Madame had called her father!

The excitement of the discovery made the blood pound in her ears, almost drowning out the soft pad of bare feet crossing the living room. Ginger heard them just in time. She lay completely still and closed her eyes. Mary peeked into the room. Satisfied, she padded softly back again. Ginger could hear the rustle of sheets through the still night, as her mother crept quietly back into her bed.

"Dear little Mommie," Ginger said softly in the darkness. "It has always been like that, all these years. She has been looking out for me, living for me, caring for me. Whatever comes in the future, she shall not be hurt. I'll see to that!"

CHAPTER THIRTEEN

HAPPINESS AND UNHAPPINESS

Mary was surprised to see Ginger coming out of her room, fully dressed, at ten o'clock the next morning. As Ginger bent to kiss her cheek, she felt a warmth that had not been there the day before. Mary had been doing some quiet, orderly thinking about their problems and was endeavoring to undo the damage which had been done—endeavoring to bring back the comradeship and understanding that they had always known as mother and daughter.

Ginger had decided that, if she must, she would tell her mother that she was going to meet her father. She hoped it would not be necessary, but, if it were necessary for any reason at all—she was ready. She had always been frank and honest with her mother. They had always met their problems together. This new antagonism which Mary had shown these last two days had not changed Ginger's faith that Mary would see things her way when she came to know Gregg, and that everything would work out happily for the three of them.

But the necessity to tell Mary where she was going was averted by Mary herself.

"Ginger, if you are going into town, will you stop at the Gray building and pay the rent?" she asked.

She did not ask why Ginger was going to town or where she might be going. Ginger realized that probably Mary guessed that she was meeting Gregg and chose to ignore it so that they might avoid an open discussion. It was so much better that way, Ginger thought.

They talked of clothes and other things and Mary stood in her usual place on the porch and smilingly watched Ginger leave the house.

It was with a strange calmness that Ginger entered the restaurant with Gregg a short time later. She was going to meet her father. This meeting might change the entire trend of her future life. It could mean trouble or it could mean happiness. She felt both a dread and a thrill of anticipation, all mixed-up together.

As Gregg checked his hat, Ginger knew a moment of sudden fright. She asked to be excused and darted hurriedly into the ladies' room. She wanted just a minute to herself before facing the difficult situation ahead. When she came out, Gregg was waiting for her.

"He isn't here yet," Gregg said.

Then, over Gregg's shoulder, Ginger saw the handsomest man she had ever seen coming toward them and smiling. Gregg followed her eyes.

"Josh!" he exclaimed.

But Josh Rogers did not hear him. He was looking at his daughter, walking directly toward her with long, young strides.

Ginger's heart leaped with joy. This man was not a stranger! She felt that she had always known and loved him. She held out first one hand, then both.

Josh took her hands in his and said simply, "My little girl."

"*Father!*" Ginger spoke his name for the first time in her life.

It seemed so natural and right. This *was* her father and she knew him instantly, with that inner knowledge born of instinct and the inexplicable ties of blood.

They had forgotten Gregg's presence until, apologetically, Josh turned to him, his arm about Ginger's waist.

"Gregg, I think this is the happiest moment of my life," he said quietly.

"Can you think of anything more wonderful than this, Josh?" Gregg cried. "Now we're going to be related. You're going to be my father-in-law."

Their faces were wreathed in smiles. The moment seemed too full and important to be spoiled by words.

Gregg led them into the dining room to the secluded table which he had reserved. They sat there, smiling, too deeply moved for speech.

When the waiter appeared with a menu, Ginger said, "How can I eat? I'm so excited!"

So Gregg ordered for the three of them—father and daughter, and the prospective son-in-law and husband.

While Gregg was ordering, her father leaned closer to Ginger.

"How is your mother?" He almost whispered the words.

"She's wonderful," Ginger answered.

For the first time she realized that Josh and her mother had been married! Once they had loved each other, as Gregg and she loved each other now. She had never before thought of Mary in connection with love and marriage.

Gregg said something to Josh and, as they talked, Ginger thought of her mother and father, together. What tragedy had separated them? They both were so fine. Perhaps it was not too late to bring them together again. If only she could bridge the chasm between them. But she made a silent vow that she would never try to force a reconciliation. She would tread softly. It was not her problem. If ever they were brought together, it must be by their own wishes and of their own volition.

"You'd better tell Josh all about it." Gregg was speaking to her and Ginger came back, startled, to the restaurant.

"About what?" she asked, bewildered.

"About Madame and Dunlop," Gregg answered.

"Do you know about Miles Harrington?" Ginger asked Josh.

"Yes. I know all about him, Ginger, and about the part you played in the incident. Gregg has told me about your experience with Dunlop, too. But, there are a few things I can't get straightened out in my mind. One is why you suspect this man, Dunlop."

Josh was smiling but his eyes were serious.

"You see, Father, I know nothing of what is behind all this. But I believe that there is spy work, sabotage, going on somewhere. Who is who in it, and what is being done, I can't figure out. Still, I know that, as sure as we're sitting here, Mr. Dunlop is mixed up in it. And, since I don't like him, I can only think of him as being one of the villains."

"I see," Josh answered, smiling indulgently. "But we can't convict him on just your feelings, Ginger. We must have concrete evidence against him."

"But I have, Father! I have!" she insisted. "Gregg thinks that his questioning me about Miles Harrington was only coincidence. I don't. I believe that he deliberately waited for me and picked me up in his car and that he hoped to question me without arousing my suspicions. As soon as I told Madame about those calls I made to New York and Florida for Mr. Dunlop, Madame went to the telephone immediately and tried to reach you. She didn't think they were merely coincidence."

Josh became very solemn.

"How do you know she tried to call me?" he asked quickly.

"Because, I heard her say 'Rogers.' For a while I thought she was giving my name. Now I know she was calling you."

Josh smiled proudly, pleased by this indication of Ginger's alertness.

"Then, in your deductions, you've cleared Madame DuLhut of any connection with the seamy side of the plot you see all about you?" he asked Ginger.

"Yes. She wouldn't have called you, unless she was

working both ends against the middle and pretending. And Madame's not that type of person. But I can't figure why she wanted so desperately to know about Miles Harrington, because, it seems to me that Miles is on the wrong side in this business, whatever it is."

Josh pursed his lips and nodded his head in understanding of the method by which Ginger had arrived at her conclusions.

"I see," he said, at last.

"I'm also pretty sure that, when we found Miles so badly injured, he was trying to get to Mr. Dunlop at the hotel. Miles didn't live there, you know," Ginger continued.

Josh's eyes twinkled. He looked at Gregg. They smiled understandingly.

"I would probably have reached the same conclusions, if I had been in your place," Josh said to Ginger.

"There are so many things you two and Mr. Bagnall know that I don't know," Ginger reminded the two men. "I'm not asking you to tell me, because I know it isn't any of my business. But strange things continue to happen and Mr. Bagnall told me to report anything I thought important."

Josh grew serious again.

"That is exactly right. If this Dunlop is up to tricks, then your switchboard will be a pretty important witness to some of it. We're already checking those calls to New York and Florida. We have the numbers from the telephone company. I expect the information to be in the office when I get back. And you are to keep your ears

Ginger Told Josh Her Deductions

wide open, Ginger, and make an instant report of anything, no matter what, if you think it is important."

She looked from one to the other of the two men.

"You two are laughing at me—I can see it," she said.
"But I don't care!"

"Indeed we're not," Josh assured her gravely. "You've
been of invaluable help to us, Ginger. Someday, maybe,
we can tell you what part you've really played in this
affair. We're only laughing because you have hit the nail
on the head so many times. I'm proud of you."

As they left the restaurant, Gregg stopped to speak to
someone who had hailed him. Father and daughter were
left alone together. Josh took Ginger's arm, as they sauntered through the front door, and said in a low voice:

"Your mother was right when she left me, Ginger. I've
never held it against her or forgiven myself and I've paid
for it dearly through all the years."

"Really, Father?" Ginger asked quickly.

"Yes. I was a spoiled boy then and didn't realize what
I was losing when I lost Mary. I soon found out. I'd give
everything I have to make it right."

"What was it, Father?"

"A silly infatuation for another woman. Didn't you
know?"

"No. Mother has never talked about you. I've never
known the reasons for your separation."

"Bless her," he said at last. "It is like her. She is a
wonderful person, your mother."

"She's more than wonderful," Ginger said in a low

voice.

There was a mist in Josh's eyes.

"Do you think—?" he began.

But he never completed the sentence because Gregg joined them at that moment.

Ginger had not decided what she would say to her mother if she should ask about her trip to town, but, as she neared the house, she decided to tell Mary the truth. There was no use putting it off. Sometime Mary would have to know that Ginger had met her father.

So, when she was home with her mother, she asked quietly:

"Mother, did you know that my father is in town—that he lives here?"

"Yes."

"I met him today."

Mary did not seem surprised.

"I knew you would, eventually," she said.

"He is a very dear friend of Gregg."

"I know that!"

Mary broke into tears and ran from the room. It was the moment she had been expecting, the moment she had tried to steel herself to face.

Ginger followed her and found Mary lying on the bed, sobbing.

"Please, Mother, this is no time for crying. It's a time for being happy. Father's such a fine man, and he's so sorry for what happened so long ago. He's waited all these years for some sign from you. He didn't say just that, in so many words, but I know he has. He still loves you. He could hardly wait for a chance to ask about you."

"He had himself transferred to this town, just to be near us. I know that, too," Mary sobbed.

"You see, Mommie, you still love *him,* too. You've been keeping track of him all these years. You've never so much as looked at another man. Don't you see?"

"Is he coming here?"

"I don't know. I didn't suggest it. We talked very little. Anyway, you two must work this out together—without my even influencing you a little bit. Do as you think best, Mommie, and don't consider me. Will you promise?"

"Yes."

Ginger dried her mother's tear-stained eyes with her handkerchief and said gaily:

"Let's fix dinner. I've got to go to work. It's getting late."

Mary smiled. Together they went to the kitchen, mother and daughter reconciled to face their problems side by side.

CHAPTER FOURTEEN

INTO ENEMY TERRITORY

Later, when Ginger left the house, a fog had rolled in from the sea, its white fingers tracing the streets and boulevards. There was a chill in the air. Ginger wrapped her coat about her, as she walked from the bus-stop to the entrance of the hotel. She was glad that Mary had insisted that she wear the coat. She'd need it even more, going home.

Patsy was waiting impatiently for Ginger to arrive. She had news to impart. Jimmy Daley had called her that afternoon and had asked to come over to her home. He'd made a terrific hit with the "fambly." Her mother thought he was "just out of this world."

And that old jalopy of his, wasn't it a peach? The gadgets he had on it beat anything Patsy had ever seen! Jimmy had stayed to dinner, too, and had met Pops. When they'd gone out in his car for ice cream for dinner, Jimmy's treat to the "fambly," he'd told her that she was his ideal type and just the kind of a girl he'd been looking for.

"Isn't it awful the way you misjudge people before you know them, Ginger?" Patsy sighed. "Now who would have thought that all this could come out of my just meeting him *here?*"

"I wouldn't be at all surprised if you and Jimmy should

marry some day," Ginger said, amused at Patsy's enthusiasm.

"Well, I will if he asks me," Patsy answered quickly.

Ginger warned, "But don't appear too anxious, Patsy. You might scare him."

"Oh, gee, you should just see the way I hold myself in," Patsy giggled.

A light came up on Patsy's board. It was Mr. Dunlop's bungalow. He didn't ask for Ginger, as he usually did.

"Connect me with George Diggens," he said.

Patsy put through the call. After it was done she turned to Ginger, who was thumbing through the daily card changes.

"Well, what d'ya know about that!" Patsy exclaimed. "That was Dunlop and he let *me* take his call. 'Spose he's sick, or something?"

"Who is he calling?"

"George Diggens, that aircraft worker in nine-eleven. Dunlop kinda gets around, doesn't he?" Patsy paused, startled by the look on Ginger's face. "What's the matter? Did I do wrong?"

"No. But how I wish I could listen to that conversation!"

"Well, open the key. Nope, you're too late. He's hung up." Patsy disconnected. "What did you wanta hear?"

"I don't know. But why would he be talking to George Diggens?"

The question was asked more of herself than of Patsy. The speculative squint in Ginger's eyes held Patsy's attention.

"I don't see why you have to be so darned ethical about everything. I'd have listened for you if you had told me to," Patsy said. "After all, how can we give people the good old Seaview service, if we don't listen once in a while? What's cookin' with that guy Dunlop, anyway? I still don't like him, you know."

"Neither do I."

"He's too soft and purring, if you ask me. What's the matter? Doesn't he like you any more?"

"Probably not."

"He didn't ask for you."

"Maybe he thought I hadn't come in yet," Ginger suggested slowly.

"Oh, that means nothing to him! He's generally on the phone twice, at least, before you come in, wondering why you aren't here yet."

"And this time he hoped I *wasn't* in yet! That's it!"

"He's a dope!" Patsy exclaimed emphatically. "Here's a ticket for you. The day chief told me to give it to you."

Ginger took the little white slip of paper and read, "The telephone company has no repair man No. 397. Please correct number. Abby."

That meant that today the telephone company had answered her inquiry of last night. There was no mistake in the number. She had checked that number with the man's badge! So the incident could mean only one thing!

"What's the matter?" Patsy asked, seeing the strange

look on Ginger's face.

"Patsy, that telephone man who was here last night wasn't employed by the telephone company at all."

"What do you mean?" Patsy demanded.

"He went to Dunlop's old suite. Then, thirty minutes later, I stood at the window and watched him come out of Dunlop's bungalow. I reported it to the night manager and he said maybe the man was lost and couldn't find his way out of the grounds. But that isn't so. He was up to something—for Mr. Dunlop."

"Up to what?" Patsy sounded annoyed as well as bewildered.

"I don't know, but I'm going to find out," Ginger answered with determination.

She plugged in on her board and Gregg answered.

"Oh, Gregg, I'm so glad you answered. There's something I didn't tell you or father about last night. I forgot and it's so awfully important."

Then she told him, almost whispering the words over the wire.

"Do you want me to call Josh, or will you? Mr. Bagnall is up in his room. Do you want to tell him?" Gregg asked, accepting her information as seriously as she had given it.

"You tell father and Mr. Bagnall. But not on the telephone, Gregg."

"I understand. Goodbye, honey. I'll call you after a while."

It was probably a half hour later that Mr. Bagnall's

signal light glowed on the board.

"Miss Rogers, will you connect me with George Diggens?" he asked.

"Yes, Mr. Bagnall."

As she listened to Mr. Bagnall's voice, Ginger had the strange feeling that a key was open—that a line was open somewhere. She glanced at Patsy's board. Patsy's key was closed. She rang George Diggens' suite, 911.

There was no response.

"He doesn't answer," she reported to Mr. Bagnall in her usual telephone voice.

"Will you keep trying, Miss Rogers? I must leave for the plant. If you find him, will you have him come over to the plant at once? I need him badly."

"Yes, Mr. Bagnall."

Ginger disconnected.

"I'll betchu that Diggens is over to Dunlop's," Patsy said hopefully.

Ginger plugged into the bungalow slot.

Dunlop answered.

"Hello. Mr. Dunlop speaking."

"Mr. Dunlop, is Mr. George Diggens with you?" Ginger asked. "He's wanted at the plant immediately."

"Oh, good evening, Miss Rogers. It's so pleasant to hear your charming voice. But I'm afraid I cannot be of any assistance to you. Sorry."

"Thank you, Mr. Dunlop," she answered quietly and disconnected.

Patsy's mouth was open as she listened and watched.

Like a flash Ginger jumped from her stool and ran to the window. As she had suspected, a man was hurrying across the lawn from Mr. Dunlop's bungalow. She ran back to the telephone, plugged the motor-court entrance and rang.

Joe answered immediately.

"Joe, there's a man coming across the lawn toward your door," Ginger said hastily. "Will you ask him if he is George Diggens? I have an important message for him. I'll hold on."

She heard Joe turn away and speak to someone. A moment later he said to her:

"Yes, Miss Rogers. He'll take the message in his room."

"Thank you," Ginger said.

So she had proved one of her conclusions! Now for one more try! But she must wait a while for that.

She gave George Diggens time enough to go up in the elevator to his room before she rang. He answered. She gave him Mr. Bagnall's message.

Now for the big try! This would prove her entire theory!

Patsy sensed the importance of what was happening.

"What are you doing?" she asked eagerly, half in a whisper.

"Ssh!" Ginger warned.

She plugged into Mr. Bagnall's apartment. She rang, her heart beating almost out of her body. If Mr. Bagnall answered, the whole plan would be ruined. She hoped he had gone as he had said. She pressed her earphone closer and listened, one hand upraised to keep Patsy silent.

She heard a click! A wire was opened! Mr. Bagnall had not answered!

Now she knew!

With her heart in her throat, almost choking her, she asked in a low, confidential, mysterious voice, "Mr. Dunlop?"

"Yes," he answered.

"Everything's okay," she whispered and instantly disconnected.

Now she knew the answer to the spurious telephone man and the answer to the open key! Mr. Dunlop had had Mr. Bagnall's telephone connected in some way to his own suite, and, when he had had to move into the bungalow, he had figured out a way to have the connection made there.

Ginger was frightened and, watching her face, Patsy's eyes were as big as dollars, too. Ginger's mind raced a mile a minute. She had let down her own barriers of defense. She had let Mr. Dunlop know that she knew! What would be his next move? Of course, the next move was his.

She must report to Gregg. She rang him, but there was no answer. He had gone to Mr. Bagnall's suite. Probably he had gone on to the plant.

Then she must call her father! She looked up the number.

Patsy was answering calls, but she was paying little attention to her work. She never took her eyes away from Ginger. And, although she talked, she heard every word Ginger said, every call she made.

Ginger made the call to her father's office number. But Josh Rogers was not in. They expected him to call in any moment, she was informed. Yes, they would give him her message.

Ginger had worked feverishly, expecting a call from the bungalow in the yard at any moment. She felt that she could almost hear that oily man deciding what to do about her.

She thought of Madame. Should she ring her? Should she tell her what she had learned? Yes, she decided. She rang. The maid answered. Madame was not in. And Madame was not in the office downstairs. Ginger felt alone, forsaken.

Where was everybody?

She looked at Patsy, as though trying to decide whether or not to take her friend into her confidence. But, remembering Patsy's excitability, she decided against it. Anyway, how could she make Patsy understand? She didn't have time to explain everything.

Intently she watched the board in front of her. If only one of her calls would come through, any one of them!

A light—there was one! No, it was the bungalow!

It was Dunlop!

Slowly she plugged in, gathering herself together as she did, swallowing hard.

It had to be faced—this was the moment!

"Yes, Mr. Dunlop," Ginger was surprised that her voice sounded so natural and so unperturbed.

"Miss Ginger, it has long been my desire to—talk to you—on a most important matter," Mr. Dunlop said in low, confidential tones.

"*Rea*-ally?" she asked with a rising inflection.

"Yes. I wonder if it might be possible tonight?"

"I get off duty so late, Mr. Dunlop," Ginger objected sensibly.

Ginger heard a key open quietly. She glanced at the other board. Patsy was listening. She motioned for Patsy to close her key. But Patsy made a face and went on listening.

"I know that," Mr. Dunlop said smoothly. "But, after tonight, that should be of little concern to you. That is, if you are a bright girl, and I think you are."

"Some people think so, Mr. Dunlop."

"May I say, in passing, that you have convinced me?" his voice insisted.

"I felt it could be done eventually, Mr. Dunlop."

She heard his dry, forced, humorless laugh.

"Then, may I expect you to join me for a—shall we say a drink—at a quiet bar? I could be waiting for you in my car on the Palisades in ten minutes."

There was no time now to hedge! It would be ruinous to change tactics! There was only one thing to do.

"I think it might be arranged, Mr. Dunlop," Ginger replied.

"That is splendid! My car will be on the far side of

the street under the palms. You know my car."

Suave satisfaction purred in his voice.

"I do, and thank you, Mr. Dunlop."

She disconnected! For one brief moment, the thing she had promised to do loomed preposterously. What was she thinking of? It was all very well to be brave when thick, brick walls and locked doors guarded you. But she was planning to go beyond their protection, to come to grips with the enemy on his own terms. Oh, why didn't somebody call—her father or Gregg or Mr. Bagnall, or even Madame?

She'd have to go through with it now. If she failed to appear, Dunlop would become alarmed, would probably escape. She held him by the slender thread of his doubt about her. If she could rise to the occasion, she could keep him around until the others were convinced, as she was, of his guilt, until her father had time to trace that telephone hook-up from Dunlop's bungalow to Mr. Bagnall's suite. Surely that would convince them all! If she played her cards well, she might get other information from him, too.

She slid down from her stool.

"Where are you going?" Patsy fairly screamed, incredulously.

Until that moment, Patsy had apparently thought that Ginger was merely joking with silly, old Dunlop.

"Patsy, now listen carefully! When my father calls—"

"Your *father!*" Patsy exclaimed, amazed.

"Well, then, when Josh Rogers calls and asks for me,

"Where Are You Going?" Patsy Fairly Screamed

tell him to trace the telephone wires from the bungalow in the yard to Mr. Bagnall's suite. Tell him I proved a hook-up. Understand?"

"No, I don't. And you're not going a step away from here." Patsy's voice was firm.

"Patsy, you've got to help. If Gregg, Mr. Bagnall, Madame, or Josh Rogers calls, give any one of them the same message."

"Ginger Rogers, you come back here!" Patsy yelled frantically.

But Ginger was gone.

Patsy promptly had hysterics. She began to cry. Her thoughts turned to the one person who was most on her mind, Jimmy.

She rang Jimmy.

"Jimmy, you gotta come down here," she said breathlessly. "Ginger's gone off with that awful Mr. Dunlop in his car, and here she is practically married to Gregg Phillips." She was sobbing. "I can't stand it another minute. She's left me here and, oh, Jimmy, I need you."

CHAPTER FIFTEEN

THE JUKE BOX

The fog had not lifted, but through it Ginger could see the familiar shape of a car standing under the palm on Palisades across from the hotel driveway. She walked up to the door. Mr. Dunlop hurried forward to help her in.

"This is most charming," he said, as he closed the door.

Now that she was here, Ginger felt no qualms. After all, this was America and this "enemy" was but a scrawny little man with an offensive, but harmless, manner. What was there to be afraid of? She would make her new-found father and her husband-to-be proud of her, because this time she would have facts, not just intuition and guesses.

"This little bar I have in mind is quiet and well appointed. I think you'll like it," Mr. Dunlop said.

"How nice. Where is it?"

"On Santa Monica Boulevard. It's called the Grotto. It's off the beaten track. Quaint. You know the type. We can get a booth and talk there undisturbed."

He was driving slowly through the fog while he talked.

Ginger stole a look at him. She did not like what she saw. The supercilious smirk was gone. In its place was a grimace, a tight-lipped, triumphant sneer.

Ginger was not as self-confident as she had been at

first.

They drove along in silence.

Finally he said, "Then you did not hear from Miles Harrington today?"

"Shall we wait until we get to the Grotto?" Ginger asked.

Mr. Dunlop smiled. Evidently he liked a battle of wits and an opponent who could hold her own. Ginger silently determined to show him, if she could, that she had a spirit and an intelligence equal, if not superior, to his.

The plowing drive through the fog ended in less than a half hour. Parking the car on a deserted street before the dimly lighted cocktail bar, advertising "A Rendez-vous for the Elite" in pale pink neon lights across its front, they went into its equally dimly-lighted interior.

Empty tables and booths told them that they were the only guests. The only other occupant of the room was the bartender. As they went in, Ginger had the impression that the bartender jumped quickly to his feet, grabbed his cloth and began polishing glasses in an effort to give the little two-by-four room some sign of life.

Ginger had not quite expected this almost complete aloneness. It gave her a momentary twinge of conscience —had she overstepped the boundaries of caution? Had she, indeed, walked foolishly into a trap?

Mr. Dunlop motioned to the booth which was the most distant from the bar. She took the side of the table facing the room. Dunlop sat opposite her, his shoulders lifted confidently.

"What will the lady have?" he asked with a mocking little bow.

"You may have what you like, but I'm going to have music," she said gaily. "The place is dead."

Before he could protest she was on her feet. She reached into her coat pocket and her fingers closed over a nickel. She inserted it into the slot of the juke box in the opposite corner.

Mr. Dunlop had half risen to follow, but changed his mind when he saw what she was doing. The bartender-waiter passed behind her and crossed the room for Mr. Dunlop's order. They talked in low voices.

The juke box was the kind which is attached to a telephone switchboard. When Ginger inserted the coin, the voice of the operator at the other end of the wire sounded clearly.

"What number do you want to hear, please?" the unseen speaker asked.

To Ginger's surprise, it was the voice of Margaret Paine, who had once worked at the Seaview Arms telephone board.

"Seaview Arms. Good evening," Ginger said in her best telephone voice.

"Why, Ginger Rogers! What are you doing there at this time of night? Is it your day off?" Margaret's amazement was vehement.

"Ssh!" Ginger cautioned. Then she added more loudly as she saw the waiter moving away from the table to the bar, "Please play 'Stardust.' I don't know the number of

it. There's no list here." She moved instantly away.

As she passed the bar, she laid a quarter in front of the bartender.

"Will you please give me some nickels?" she asked.

Hesitantly the man made the change, with a sharp, sidewise glance at Mr. Dunlop.

Ginger reached the table as the lovely strains of her selection poured forth from the juke box.

"Very nice music," Mr. Dunlop said. "But you should have let me do it."

At that same moment a light glowed on Patsy's board in the far-off Seaview Arms.

"Seaview Arms. Good evening." Patsy answered, choking back her sobs of fear and anxiety over Ginger's sudden departure to meet Mr. Dunlop.

"Patsy!" It was Margaret Paine. "What is Ginger doing down at the Grotto Bar?"

"Is *that* where she is?" Patsy began to cry like a small child. "I'm going to tell her mother. Margaret, something's going on! Ginger's gone off with an awful man. Why, he might even kill her! I wouldn't put anything past that man."

"That Grotto is an awful place!" Margaret cried, catching Patsy's excitement. "A dive! All sorts of shady things happen there. Don't you think you should send somebody down there after her?"

"There's nobody to send until Jimmy gets here," Patsy sobbed. "Jimmy's a friend of mine. But how did you know where she went?"

"She called me on the juke. When I answered, she said, 'Seaview Arms. Good evening.' That's how I knew it was Ginger. I'm playing 'Stardust' for her now."

"Well, don't play anything more. Make her call back, then ask her if she needs help. I'm scared to death, Margaret," Patsy cried excitedly.

"I'll keep you posted," Margaret said and rang off.

Patsy rang Ginger's house. Mary answered.

"Oh, Mrs. Rogers, something terrible has happened!" Patsy's voice trembled. "Ginger's gone off with a man, a horrible man. She's down at an awful place, a regular dive, with him right now. And she's in danger! He might kill her, Mrs. Rogers."

"Patsy, what are you talking about?" Mary almost screamed.

"It's a terrible dive, Mrs. Rogers. And that man's a murderer. Ginger's caught him in something, I don't know what, and she—"

Patsy heard Mary call, "Josh, Josh, come here!"

In a moment a cool, quiet, masculine voice spoke to Patsy.

"Will you repeat to me what you've just told Mrs. Rogers?"

"Oh, yes. Are you *Josh* Rogers?"

"Yes."

"Ginger left a message for you at your office and she said when you called here I was to tell you—oh, what was it? I can't think!" Patsy stammered frantically.

Josh said, "Now go slowly and be sure to give me all

the details. It will save time, in the end."

Patsy took a deep breath and tried to speak calmly.

"Ginger talked to that Mr. Dunlop and made a date with him and went away with him. She walked right out of the telephone room here just as though she didn't have a job or nothing. Just before she went she said if Josh Rogers or Gregg or Mr. Bagnall called, I was to tell them to trace the telephone wires—oh, now let me see . . . It was something about the bungalow in the yard and Mr. Bagnall's suite here in the hotel."

"Why did she want us to trace the wires? Now be calm, Miss. It will save time."

"She said—she'd proved a hook-up, whatever that means."

"How did you find out where she is? Did she tell you where she was going?"

"No. I found out by accident. The juke box operator telephoned in. Ginger had called for a number from that awful Grotto on Santa Monica. When Margaret answered, Ginger said, 'Seaview Arms. Good evening,' and that's how Margaret knew who she was. So Margaret called me—and I called Mrs. Rogers."

"You did exactly right! Now if Mr. Phillips or Mr. Bagnall calls in, give him her message, will you?" Josh hung up abruptly.

Miles away in the Grotto, Ginger toyed with her glass, pretending to drink. Mr. Dunlop saw what she was doing.

"You don't have to drink it, if you don't want it," he said indulgently.

"I never drink, Mr. Dunlop," Ginger replied quickly. "We came here to talk. Hadn't we better begin?"

"Yes. First, we must straighten out the matter of Miles Harrington. You will tell me now what you know about that." He smiled with mock encouragement.

Ginger leaned across the table and looked him squarely in the eyes. "You underrate me, Mr. Dunlop," she said quietly.

"Meaning—?"

"We are not playing games. A man in your position must know everything so closely related to himself and his work. Why should I tell *you,* even if I did know?"

"You are very direct, young woman. I like that."

"I don't think you do."

"Well—that is—" he stammered uncertainly. "Well, we're not going to get on very speedily this way. Just why did you think I wanted to talk with you?"

"I won't mince words," Ginger said clearly. "I thought you had seen the light and wanted me to work with you —intelligently."

"Oh, I see! You imagined I—"

"I never imagine, Mr. Dunlop. After all, don't you think your pretending at this stage of the game is just a little childish?"

"Perhaps. But then, I am dealing with a child. You are very clever, Miss Rogers, but quite obvious, at times."

"May I return the compliment?" She bowed her head derisively.

The music from the juke box had come to a close.

With birdlike swiftness Ginger was on her feet.

"At least, we can have more music," she called over her shoulder, as she hurried toward the box.

Dunlop rose slowly as Ginger dropped her nickel in the box.

Margaret opened her key at once, as though she had been waiting for the call. But, before she could answer, Ginger put her mouth close to the box and whispered, "D.A." In telephone language, understood by operators, that meant, "They don't answer."

Margaret was quick. She understood Ginger's whispered signal to mean, "Don't answer." She kept her key open and listened.

Dunlop sauntered up to the machine. The bartender had left the room. Ginger and Mr. Dunlop were alone.

"What are we going to hear this time?" he asked.

"So far as I'm concerned, Mr. Dunlop, I've heard enough. If you feel the same way, we can call it a day."

Dunlop leaned an elbow on the juke box.

"But *I* haven't heard enough and I like this place and the company," he said meaningly.

"This would be a nice place for a murder," Ginger said distinctly as she smiled back. "I see the bartender has conveniently disappeared. So, if you happen not to like the color of my hair or eyes—well, the whole thing would be comparatively easy."

Mr. Dunlop laughed suavely and mockingly.

"It is hardly as bad as that," he said. "Still I'm afraid that I can't permit you to tear yourself away without informing me of the whereabouts of Miles Harrington."

Ginger did not flinch. Somehow, she felt as if she had been prepared for this moment.

"In other words, Mr. Dunlop, you are telling me that I shall not be permitted to leave here until I have told you all I know," she said calmly.

"That is a bit blunt, my dear, but you have the general idea."

"I see. Then may I tell you that you are a very stupid little man?"

Ginger was angry. Mr. Dunlop's smile, the satisfied grin of a slinking cat playing with a helpless little mouse, enraged her. She wasn't helpless. She had the juke box as her concealed weapon, her protection. Mr. Dunlop knew nothing about that.

"You are handling this as stupidly as you did the Miles Harrington matter!" she exclaimed.

It was a shot in the dark, but it hit the mark. Mr. Dunlop sobered. The mocking smile left his face.

Silently Ginger hoped that Margaret was listening and that she was able to understand what she was hearing. Everything depended upon Margaret's intelligence, her ability to interpret what she heard into action.

"Let's drop all this silly subterfuge, Mr. Dunlop, and get down to cases," Ginger went on in a clear voice. "Are you willing to pay well for the information you need, the information, which you should already know? Is it worth money to you to cover up your own inefficiency?"

"I am ready to pay. What is your price?"

Mr. Dunlop's entire demeanor had suddenly changed. He had dropped the mask of a scholarly gentleman. He was even talking with rough harshness out of the corner of his mouth.

The change startled Ginger. She knew that now she was facing the real Mr. Dunlop and she felt a sudden, tense fear. This man was a killer, capable of doing anything to gain his ends. He was determined to know what she knew. He had no intention of paying any price whatever for that knowledge. Ginger shuddered, looking at his cold, implacable eyes. She must play for time.

"What's your price?" Mr. Dunlop repeated.

"I'll have to think about that," Ginger said with pretended lightness. "Shall we have some music while we barter? There's a new number, just out. It's called, 'Margaret, Call the F.B.I.' The tune is catchy and the words go, *'Margaret call the F.B.I. and tell them all you've heard.'"*

As she spoke, she turned her head slightly so that she was speaking almost directly into the mouthpiece of the juke box.

"But maybe you wouldn't like that tune, Mr. Dunlop," she added, turning back to him.

As she turned, she heard the faraway click of the key on Margaret's board. Her knees fairly sagged under her with her thrilled relief. Margaret had understood!

With trembling fingers she reached into her pocket for another nickel. But, as she lifted her hand toward the coin slot, Mr. Dunlop grabbed it. She looked up at him,

"What's Your Price?" Mr. Dunlop Repeated

questioningly.

"I don't know what you're up to, but I don't like it!" he rasped, hurting her hand with the rough strength of his grip.

Ginger pulled her fingers from his grasp.

"We might as well get this straight right at the beginning, Mr. Dunlop," she said. "I'm not afraid of you or anything you can do!"

In her anger, she threw all caution to the winds, forgetting that, at best, she could not expect help from Margaret's alarm before at least half an hour had passed.

"I wouldn't tell you anything!" she exclaimed. "You're a traitor and a saboteur and a Fifth Columnist! You're trying to sell out my country to our enemies! I know all about you, Mr. Dunlop! But your game's over! My father will take care of you!"

The outburst was so totally unexpected that Mr. Dunlop gasped like a fish out of water. Then, as he realized the full meaning of Ginger's words, fear gripped him in a frenzy. His panic drove all reason from his brain. His long, bony hand darted out like the talon of a pouncing eagle and closed over Ginger's shoulder.

Ginger wrenched her shoulder free, only to find his claw-like fingers fastened in the sleeve of her coat. She wriggled out of the coat and, in the struggle which followed, her face was close to his. She could see the bulging, glassy stare of his eyes, the mad eyes of a man gone berserk.

Then his mouth opened and he uttered a low, hoarse

call. Looking over his shoulder, Ginger saw a door open behind the bar. And through the door walked the ugly, little man she had seen in the theater that night with Miles, the man who had switched the packages of cigarettes when Miles had dropped his package.

The next few minutes were a dim, hazy confusion to Ginger. Desperately she struggled against the two men, who grasped her arms with fingers of steel. She was pinioned from both sides. Strong, rough fingers dug deeply into the flesh of her arms and shoulders. She was quite helpless against the strength of Dunlop and the newcomer.

Then she heard the thunder of blows on the front door of the cafe.

"The door must be locked. Whoever is there can't get in," she thought vaguely, as she struggled frantically to free herself from the iron strength of the two men who held her prisoner.

Kicking and fighting, she was pulled and hauled through the opening behind the bar and toward the rear of the building. The pounding on the front door grew louder and more insistent as she was pushed through another door and into a dark passage. She tried to dig her heels into the floor to stop her forward rush. She turned and twisted and fought. But the strength of the two men was too much for her even to struggle against.

They reached another door. One of the men released an arm to open it. With a swift lurch Ginger almost jerked herself free. But the next moment four strong hands clutched her again and she was pushed through the door into the darkness of the outdoors.

She saw the dim outline of an automobile standing a few feet away. She was being forced relentlessly toward the car.

Then something happened. With a startling suddenness the struggle was over. Without uttering a word, the two men released her. She staggered forward, almost falling with the unexpected swiftness of her release.

She regained her balance and turned. Two men stood behind her two assailants whose arms were slowly reaching upward. As Ginger's bewildered eyes became accustomed to the darkness, she saw more clearly the dim outline of one of the newcomers and recognized Josh Rogers.

"Father, is that you?" Ginger cried.

"Yes, Ginger. Get behind me. These birds might want to make a break for it and save the government a lot of expense."

CHAPTER SIXTEEN

THE RIDDLE ANSWERED

As Ginger watched, still dazed with excitement, the three criminals, Mr. Dunlop, the ugly little man, and the bartender, were pushed into a car in the custody of two of Josh Rogers' husky assistants. Then Josh led Ginger to a second car and helped her into the rear seat.

Ginger stared with unbelieving eyes when she saw her mother sitting in the car. Numb with the exciting happenings of the last few hours, Ginger sat beside her mother and moved to make room for her father on her other side, before she suddenly realized that her mother's presence must mean that, somehow, somewhere, there had been a reconciliation between her parents. Then, without speaking, she put an arm around each one and the two persons now so dear pressed happily close to her.

The two automobiles moved forward toward the city and the F.B.I. headquarters. The car in which Ginger rode followed the one which held the three prisoners and their guards. The three in the second car rode in silence, their fingers interlocked, their hearts too full for words.

Suddenly, as they rolled toward the heart of the city, Ginger realized that another car was moving beside them and that a voice was calling to them. Quickly Josh lowered the window.

"Hey, give me my girl!" Gregg Phillips called from the other car.

Smiling, Josh told the driver to stop. Ginger dashed out and into Gregg's car. The two cars moved forward to catch up with the one ahead and the little procession drove on.

Gregg aimed a kiss at Ginger's face, planting it on the tip of her nose.

"You've got more courage than good sense, Ginger Rogers," he scolded affectionately. "You really should be spanked and sent to bed without your supper. You had the right idea about that guy Dunlop all along and you sewed him in a bag when you discovered that hook-up from his bungalow to Mr. Bagnall's suite, but you shouldn't have gone off alone with him. You should have got hold of me. Then your Dad and I could have done the rest."

"I know I should," Ginger laughed. "But you two didn't believe me. I had to keep track of him after he found out I knew, until you traced the hook-up and were convinced of his guilt."

"I told Josh that we should have explained to you at lunch that we agreed with your hunch about Dunlop, but he thought it best not to let you know. We didn't dream that anything as important as all this would happen today," Gregg said seriously. "We thought it would take a little time. But, look!"

He paused and pointed to a pile of telephone paraphernalia on the shelf of his car behind the seat.

"All those telephone instruments and wires and gadgets came out of Dunlop's bungalow. We have everything we need to hang him, except the rope. And you did it, you silly little good-lookin'!"

They laughed together, thrilled, excited, happy and gay.

Another surprise was waiting for Ginger when she walked into the F.B.I. offices with her mother, her father, and Gregg. Miles Harrington was sitting in the office, his head swathed in bandages. And beside him, tenderly touching his injured head, stood Madame DuLhut, smiling tenderly.

Madame looked years older. The smile which she turned to Ginger was almost tearful in its sadness. Her shoulders drooped and mental anguish had imprinted lines of age on her once smooth face.

"Madame! What are you doing here?" Ginger cried anxiously, crossing the room to stand beside Madame DuLhut.

Quickly Ginger glanced toward her father and Gregg, hoping for an explanation. The smiles on their faces brought relief to her heart.

"ZheeZhee, zees funnee Miles ees my grandson, Millen Hariot," Madame said. "I deed not even know he was in zees countree. How am I to know that Miles Harrington ees Millen Hariot? Two days ago I learn he ees here. Meester Bagnall tells me. But he weel not tell me where he ees nor what happen to heem. I tried to get you to tell me, but you are too smart, ZheeZhee."

Madame put her arm around Ginger and hugged her affectionately.

"Did Mr. Dunlop know that Miles was your grand-son?" Ginger asked, a little of the mystery beginning to clear.

"He has known all zees time," Madame answered. "He nevaire tell me. He has been using my boy, for hees sabotage. When Miles was hurt, Meester Bagnall took heem to zee home of hees brother, who is a doctaire. The doctaire cared for my poor Millen."

Ginger and Madame turned as Josh Rogers led Miles across the room to face the three prisoners, who were standing against the wall, their faces sullen and downcast. Their two husky guards stood beside them. Josh spoke in a low voice to Miles. Miles answered in a whisper, pointing to the bartender and the ugly little man. Then Josh signaled the guards and they shoved the three captives out of the room.

As Josh and Miles turned back toward the three women, who were now standing close together in a watchful silence, Mr. Bagnall hurried into the room. His hands were filled with papers and there was a leather portfolio under his arm. He walked directly to Ginger and took her hand as best he could.

"You did a wonderful job, my dear!" he said warmly.

Then the smiling Josh joined them. He reached for Mary's hand and pulled her to his side.

"I want you to meet my wife, Bagnall," he said proudly. "Mary, may I present Mr. Bagnall?"

Ginger looked at her mother and saw the new radiance which overspread her face. Mary looked years younger. Her eyes glowed with a young and happy light.

Ginger sighed with happiness. Her eyes sought Gregg's and they smiled in silent understanding.

Then Ginger's eyes saw a gleam of scarlet on a desk near the window. She rushed over to it.

It was her scarlet opera cloak! It had not been cleaned. Bits of broken leaves still clung to it and its crimson sheen was darkened by blood stains. It lay bunched in a neglected mass.

Ginger's eyes softened as she looked at it. This scarlet cloak had meant so much in her life. It had led her into exciting and dangerous adventures. It had brought her to Gregg, whom she now knew and loved. Through the cloak she had found her father. It had reunited her mother and father.

But where had the scarlet cloak come from in the beginning?

"Do you know yet who sent this cloak to me, Father?" Ginger asked, her fingers gently caressing the exquisite material of the mysterious garment.

"Yes, my dear. Mr. Dunlop sent it to you," Josh answered. "You see, Mr. Dunlop manipulated his ring of spies and saboteurs in a strange way. He did not let them know each other. He kept them apart, their identities secret from each other. So, when he wanted one to contact another, he had to arrange some way for them to identify each other.

"This scarlet cloak was one of the means of identification. Miles was to meet another Dunlop henchman at the theater. They were to exchange cigarette packages. So, in order that the other man might recognize him, Miles was to take a girl to the theater and the girl was to wear this scarlet cloak. The cloak was the signal for the exchange of the cigarettes. In Miles's package was the supposed plan of the new bombsight. In the other man's package was five thousand dollars, as payment for the plan."

"Then Miles was——?" Ginger began, bewildered at this explanation.

"Just a minute, my dear," her father smiled. "Miles was working for me through Mr. Bagnall while he was posing as one of Dunlop's henchmen. I didn't know until that afternoon that you were the girl who was to wear the cloak. Then I was nearly crazy, but it was too late to stop the plans. We had arranged to close in and grab them that night. I guess it was my over-anxiety about you that made me let them slip through my fingers.

"They discovered that the plan for the bombsight was a fake soon after they left the theater. They risked everything to come back to get Miles. They lured him away from the restaurant, as you know, took the money away from him and thought that they had killed him. Then, when they didn't read of the discovery of his body the next day, they knew that something had gone wrong. They tried desperately to find out what had happened.

They knew that, if Miles were alive, he could identify the man at the theater and the others, so eventually we would get them. If he were dead, they could go on with their work, unmolested. Understand?"

"Yes," Ginger nodded. "The ugly little man was the one in the theater."

"I know. Miles just told me. And the bartender was the man who almost killed Miles and left him for dead. George Diggens was another one of Dunlop's men. We got him tonight. But, in spite of our efforts, we couldn't get a line on the man higher up. You did that, Ginger! You suspected him! You trapped him! I'll never laugh at your intuition again as long as I live! I certainly shall not!"

Josh put his arms around his daughter and hugged her proudly.

"What goes on here?" Gregg asked, as he walked over to join them.

"I've been explaining the recent happenings to Ginger," Josh said.

"But I still don't quite understand where Gregg fits into the picture," Ginger smiled.

"Gregg has been working with me for some time," Josh told her.

"And now we'll both be working for you," Gregg cried, putting his arm around Ginger.

Ginger looked from her father to the man she loved.

"If it hadn't been for the scarlet cloak, I might never have found the real you, Gregg," Ginger whispered, looking up at him with glowing eyes.

"You can never make me believe that we wouldn't have found each other someway, Ginger," Gregg whispered tenderly.

WHITMAN
AUTHORIZED EDITIONS

NEW STORIES OF ADVENTURE AND MYSTERY

Up-to-the-minute novels for boys and girls about Favorite Characters, all popular and well-known, including—

INVISIBLE SCARLET O'NEIL
LITTLE ORPHAN ANNIE and the Gila Monster Gang
BRENDA STARR, Girl Reporter
DICK TRACY, Ace Detective
DICK TRACY Meets the Night Crawler
TILLIE THE TOILER and the Masquerading Duchess
BLONDIE and Dagwood's Adventure in Magic
BLONDIE and Dagwood's Snapshot Clue
BLONDIE and Dagwood's Secert Service
JOHN PAYNE and the Menace at Hawk's Nest
BETTY GRABLE and the House With the Iron Shutters
BOOTS (of "Boots and Her Buddies") and the Mystery of the Unlucky Vase
ANN SHERIDAN and the Sign of the Sphinx
JUDY GARLAND and the Hoodoo Costume

WHITMAN
AUTHORIZED EDITIONS

THE EXCITING
FIGHTERS FOR FREEDOM
SERIES

Thrilling novels of war and adventure for modern boys and girls

Kitty Carter of the CANTEEN CORPS

Nancy Dale, ARMY NURSE

March Anson and Scoot Bailey of the U.S. NAVY

Dick Donnelly of the PARATROOPS

Norma Kent of the WACS

Sally Scott of the WAVES

Barry Blake of the FLYING FORTRESS

Sparky Ames and Mary Mason of the FERRY COMMAND

The books listed above may be purchased at the same store where you secured this book.